12/10 DR   20

D1462232

A TIME TO GROW

HOME TO HEATHER CREEK

A TIME To GROW

Robert Elmer

Guideposts
NEW YORK, NEW YORK

www.guideposts.com
(800) 932-2145
Guideposts Books & Inspirational Media

Cover by Lookout Design, Inc.
Interior design by Cindy LaBreacht
Typeset by Nancy Tardi

Printed in the United States of America
10 9 8 7 6 5 4 3 2 1

Acknowledgments

This story is dedicated to my in-laws, Ron and Robin. In their compassion and in their consistent efforts with six kids they very practically demonstrated Proverbs 22:6: "training up children in the way they should go." Years later, the ripple effect of their faithfulness continues . . . to grandchildren and beyond.

—Robert Elmer

Home to Heather Creek

A TIME TO GROW

Chapter One

How very odd.

Charlotte Stevenson stood by the mailbox late on a chilly Thursday afternoon, braving a cold April breeze that rustled what remained of last fall's corn stubble and tousled her hair. Leaving her blue knit sweater unbuttoned, she turned the envelope from their next-door neighbor over and over in her hand.

If Walt Freeman had wanted to tell us something, she thought, *he might have just stepped over here and told us himself.* Instead, he had gone to all the trouble of writing, addressing, and stamping a letter that ultimately traveled all of a quarter mile.

Charlotte had to admit the envelope did look quite official; it was addressed to "Robert Stevenson" and printed on fancy white stationery that crinkled in her hands. She held it up for a moment to make out the watermark while hoping the leaden gray sky wouldn't release another downpour. Too anxious to wait until she got inside to see what the envelope contained, Charlotte carefully opened the seal and unfolded the letter inside. As she glanced over the words, she had no trouble understanding Walt's intent.

He made his point abundantly clear with straight-backed phrases like "it has come to my attention" and "you are hereby notified." Perhaps he had picked up the verbiage from a how-to book explaining the steps for suing your next-door neighbor. Still, she read every hurtful word just to be sure her eyes weren't playing tricks.

"I would like to avoid getting county officials involved in a stop-work order," she read in a whisper. "But since it has come to my attention that Pete's home-building has encroached upon my property, I will have no choice but to pursue legal action if you do not voluntarily relocate said building forthwith."

Said building forthwith? Goodness gracious! Despite Walt's stilted legalese, his threat remained clear. In fact he was obviously good and riled up about this, and the men needed to know right away—Bob and Pete both.

Charlotte headed back down their gravel driveway toward Heather Creek Farm, shaking from the chill for the first time. Or perhaps from something else. She remembered the "something else" when she saw the dark house.

Bob isn't home. He would have to deal with it as soon as he returned home from Christopher's 4-H meeting.

Neither is Pete. She had to remind herself that their son didn't live with them anymore. He and Dana would be home from their short honeymoon any day now.

"Oh, Pete!" she muttered, stepping onto the back porch with the unwelcome mail clutched in one hand. "What did you do?"

In the dim circle of pale gold light she could see Toby coming in from her walk, which was good. The old dog really needed to stay close and not wander the newly plowed fields. There was no telling what kind of small animal she might come upon, and Charlotte was in no mood to deal with the aftereffects of a Toby-versus-skunk or Toby-versus-raccoon encounter. She'd had to deal with those situations a time or two. On a Nebraska farm there was no avoiding such things.

She stepped inside and then let Toby in too. "Hey, old girl. It's about time you made it back," she said.

Toby greeted Charlotte with an enthusiastic wag of her tail and promptly plunked herself down on the worn kitchen linoleum to scratch an ear.

At least now Charlotte had someone to talk to. Emily hadn't yet returned from her friend Ashley's house, where they were supposedly studying for a math test.

Sam was "out." Just out. Presumably with Jake and Paul. At least he knew he had to be back in by ten on a school night. But as the spring of his senior year in high school warmed up, that curfew was getting harder and harder to enforce.

She did know that Christopher, the baby of the family at twelve, was safe with his grandpa at their 4-H meeting. Still, she wished they would hurry back. She laid the letter on the worn kitchen table where Bob wouldn't miss it.

Seeking the comfort of routine, she collected the ingredients for her famous chocolate chip cookies. At the counter, she added eggs to her recipe, one at a time, and then the chocolate chips and nuts. Still, something seemed to be missing; she thought through the process the same way she did when she couldn't remember the name of someone new at church. The right ingredients? Yes. In the right order? Naturally. So what was different this time?

She pulled out a couple of baking sheets and proceeded to spoon out a pattern of dough dollops.

And then it occurred to her.

"You know what's wrong, Toby?" she asked the dog, who had curled up on a towel by the back door, next to the pile of boots. Toby whacked her tail on the floor and then whimpered in obvious sympathy.

Toby knew. Even though Pete would still arrive on the farm every day to work with his father, he didn't live here anymore. He wouldn't track mud into the kitchen every night, stopping to chat with his mom about the weather or the trouble they were having with their old tractor again or the sick horse.

And he wouldn't stop in after dinner to tell a dumb joke before he scarfed down half the contents of the cookie jar so she couldn't pretend to get upset at him or scold him. At the moment she wished more than anything that she could.

She shouldn't be like this. She tried not to sniffle as she prepared a second sheet of cookies and set her egg timer. She should be happy for them.

She *was* happy for them. Overjoyed. Pete was a good man. A little wise-talking, perhaps, and sometimes not as careful as he should be, but who didn't have some faults? Pete was gentle and always so good with the kids—maybe because he was still a big kid himself. But no one could say he was not hardworking, and he was always looking to upgrade the farm or improve their operation. He had promised Dana a new home, and now it was getting underway.

She wondered what had gone wrong. And now how were they going to deal with the challenge from Walt

Freeman? Was Pete really building his place in the wrong spot? For his sake, she certainly hoped not.

For a moment Charlotte thought of calling up Pete's number and leaving him a message. He should be aware of this as soon as possible. Instead she checked the Bedford Feed & Seed calendar tacked to the wall next to the refrigerator, counting the days since the wedding.

Two, three . . . OK. Only five days had passed since they went away. If the kids had left before lunch today they might have arrived home at Dana's little house in Bedford after their brief honeymoon at that bed and breakfast on the river. Or they might still be driving back. Either way, she would give them a chance to get home before hitting them with the bad news.

The egg timer pinged, and she reached for a potholder to grab the corner of the first cookie sheet. She must have splashed the pad with dishwater somewhere along the line; the heat nipped her fingers through the wet potholder, and she nearly dumped the entire first batch on the floor.

"Ow!" she wailed. She dropped the tray onto the stovetop, slipped the second batch into the oven, and then stuck her fingers under a stream of cold water. One would think that after all these years of baking cookies, she might be better at avoiding disasters.

She leaned against the counter, allowing the cold water to wash over her throbbing fingers as she held back tears—of pain, yes, but also for the loss of her baby.

Her thirty-four-year-old baby.

"What's wrong with me, Toby?" she asked her dog, but Toby must have heard something outside. She trotted to the back door, ignoring the clatter of the cookie sheet. She woofed and whined as a car rolled down the gravel driveway from Heather Creek Road and pulled into a parking spot just outside.

"Oh, good," Charlotte said, wiping her hands on her apron. The throbbing from her little burn had mainly subsided by now. "They're home."

Moments later Christopher poked his head in the back door, his cheeks rosy with excitement. Forty-degree wind rushed in past him, bearing scents of fertilizer and seed and newly plowed fields.

"Grandma!" His eyes danced. "Come out here, quick! You've got to see!"

"See?" Charlotte plucked a sweater off the coat tree, wondering what had her grandson so worked up. "See what?"

Christopher didn't answer; he had already run back out, leaving her to follow as best she could. Toby launched out on her own, barking herself silly.

"Toby, no!" Christopher tried to grab the dog, but it was too late. The dog had spotted his little lamb, still in Bob's arms. He swiped at the dog again.

Bob was struggling to hold onto the panicky, squirming animal, but Toby must have caught him off guard, and the bleating lamb kicked his way free and landed on the driveway. It struggled to right itself, and then ran straight for the barn, away from the dog, whose herding instinct had abruptly kicked in.

Christopher sprinted after the frightened little lamb, followed by Charlotte, her apron flapping. They all yelled at Toby to call off the chase.

"Toby, come back here!" yelled Christopher.

"Toby, you mangy mutt!" Bob yelled even more loudly as he grabbed a flashlight from the cab of his truck and joined the parade.

"Toby, please!" Charlotte decided pleading might be in order.

No matter which way they tried, Toby wasn't listening; they all followed the desperate bleating and barking through the barn's open door. Now Bob's flashlight broke into the darkness with a narrow beam, framing bales of hay, rusty tractor attachments, and a lamb forced into the far corner with Toby dancing in circles in front of him.

"There he is!" yelled Christopher, rushing over to the dog. "Toby, chill out!"

Toby wasn't about to calm down, though, especially not when she had the object of her herding efforts in her sights. Christopher and Bob nearly had to tackle the dog, pulling her back from where she had adeptly cornered the poor lamb. That left Charlotte to come up behind the lamb, grabbing it gently by the shank with one hand and slipping an arm around its shoulder and neck.

"Whoa, Grandma." Christopher sounded impressed. "How did you know how to do that?"

The little lamb wasn't very heavy, and she carried him in her arms past the excited Toby.

"You'll learn," she answered. "Now, where do you want the little guy?"

Bob and Christopher had prepared a small pen on the other side of the barn, secure with fine-mesh wire and complete with a little doghouse type of shelter. They would have to make sure the actual dog didn't come near, although by now it appeared Toby was finally settling down.

"We're going to have to make sure the lamb doesn't get loose, aren't we?" she told them, setting it down inside the pen.

Christopher held Toby by the collar. They would still need to give the lamb a food bowl, clean water, and probably straw or shavings to keep his pen clean.

"The little fella just squirmed out of my grip before I even knew what was going on, with the dog and all," Bob explained.

"It wasn't Grandpa's fault," said Christopher, keeping an eye on the lamb. The little black creature was still shaking from the misadventure.

"I'm not saying it was anyone's fault." Charlotte hadn't meant it that way. She pulled her husband back, lowering her voice. "Bob, there's something important I need to tell you."

Chapter Two

A steady rain fell on the highway ahead, and Pete squinted to see through the weather as he fiddled with the variable wiper control on Dana's Honda. *Their* Honda. He still wasn't quite used to driving anything newer than thirty years old that wasn't a truck. He glanced over at his bride and smiled at the way she moved her head.

"Dana." He touched her arm, causing her to catch her breath. "We're almost home."

Home. He liked the sound of that word, realizing it now meant something entirely different than it had the first thirty-three years of his life. For a moment the flash of passing headlights etched her soft features in his mind: the round face with bangs fringed on the forehead, the cute little button nose, the crinkles around the corners of her eyes that stood out when she laughed. He'd discovered a new appreciation for that laugh over the past few days during their honeymoon at the river.

"Dana, come on." He wiggled her elbow this time until she finally straightened up and stretched her neck and arms.

"Home?" She blinked and sucked in a breath of air. "How long have I been sleeping?"

Pete steered around a puddle from a backed-up drain at the edge of town.

"Since about York—the last hour or so."

She acted surprised that she had slept so long, but Pete hadn't minded doing the driving, even through the rain. He just let his pleasant honeymoon memories replay in his mind as they made their way across miles of Nebraska fields, most now plowed and ready for planting corn.

Dad would need help with the planting very soon.

I wonder if Brad got the new starter we ordered for the tractor. It's been three weeks; it ought to be here by now. And what about the plowing?

He wasn't at all sure how his dad had managed over the past few days by himself, considering his age and his health. He'd find out in the morning, though.

"Pete?" Dana broke into his thoughts as they turned onto Oldham Street only two blocks from Dana's—*their*—little house.

"Huh?" He glanced over at her. "Did you say something?"

"I said, you're going to sleep in tomorrow morning, aren't you? You don't have to wake up at four AM."

"Oh. Actually, I was thinking of checking in on Dad in the morning, and—"

"Peter Charles Stevenson! We're on our honeymoon, for heaven's sake, and I don't have to be at work until Monday. Surely you can at least sleep in and go out to the farm tomorrow afternoon."

"But I'm not going back to work, exactly. Just checking

up on a couple of things, making sure we're on track. I'll be back early."

Dana groaned as they pulled into the driveway, and Pete knew she wasn't finished with him yet.

"'Back early' isn't quite what I had in mind, honey."

"B-but ..." He stuttered as a new downpour nearly drowned them out. "Dana, I just can't sit around here on my duff while Dad is out there doing all the work. I told him I'd be back in time to help with the plowing, and for sure the planting. We should be ready."

"That's not what you told me." She turned so she was facing him.

"I'm sorry. Look. We can go out to dinner tomorrow. How about that? You don't have to cook, if that's what you're worried about."

"What's that supposed to mean?" She crossed her arms over her chest. "Already you don't like my cooking?"

"No! That's not what I meant at all. I'm just saying that if you still want to be on our honeymoon, we can still be on our honeymoon. Sort of."

"Yeah—if you call a honeymoon sitting home alone while my husband is off driving his tractor around the fields."

"Not going to be driving the tractor tomorrow with all this rain." Pete pulled the key out of the ignition. "But you're going to have to get used to the fact that your husband does that sort of thing for a living."

"I'm well aware of what my husband does for a living. I was just hoping we'd be able to have a normal honeymoon, like most couples."

"Most couples live in the suburbs. Most couples have a 401(k) and two weeks of paid vacation. Most couples spend two hours a day commuting to their offices. Do you really want to be like most couples?"

Instantly he regretted the tone of voice he'd used. Dana didn't answer right away, and he bailed out of the car to open the garage door. Soaked by the rain, he fiddled with the key by the illumination of their headlights, vowing to trade in as many wedding presents as it took to get an automatic garage door opener. How many sets of mixing bowls did a guy need anyway?

When he got back to the car Dana had already hopped out. He hurriedly parked the Honda in the little detached, single-car garage, common to the 1940s–style cottages in this part of town.

"Hey, wait!" he called as he hurried out of the garage and followed Dana to the front step under the little overhang. He would apologize now and unpack later.

Dana fumbled with her set of keys in the dark; the only light filtered through the lilac bushes from the next-door neighbor's place. Usually the Millers retired early, but they were up later tonight. It was nearly ten o'clock.

In what he hoped was one smooth move, Pete reached over with his own key, unlocked the door, and shoved it open. At the same time, he caught Dana under the arm with one arm and scooped under her knees with the other. He would either sweep her off her feet or they'd both collapse on the front step. He hoped for the former.

"Pete!" Dana protested, but she needn't have bothered. "What in the world are you doing?"

"What do you think I'm doing?" He held her as high as

he dared. "I'm sorry for raising my voice and acting like a Neanderthal farmer. Plus, I'm carrying you across the threshold, the way husbands are supposed to do."

"A Neanderthal, huh? Well, I wouldn't have used that word exactly."

"What word would you have used then?"

"Maybe we should just let it go at that. Apology accepted. That *was* an apology, wasn't it?"

"You got it. But I'm going to need to put you down."

She giggled as he charged through the door, turning so they'd both fit through it, and then he gently deposited her on the couch.

"Thank you, sir."

He was relieved that they were home, and he hoped she'd forget their disagreement about honeymoon time versus farm time. He also hoped it wasn't the first of many such discussions, because Dana was going to have to get used to the hours a farmer had to put in. He thought she understood, but when it came down to it, he knew it was harder than she had imagined. He bent down a little closer for a kiss, but she sat up straight.

"What?" he asked.

"The answering machine is beeping." She popped up. "We'd better see who called."

Pete groaned but followed her into the kitchen. At least they'd updated the answering message to say, "You've reached Pete and Dana Stevenson's place . . ."

Dana played back the messages, beginning with an automated voice from a loan company, informing them that interest rates had hit an all-time low. Next was Dana's college roommate Judy, who was "so bummed out" that she hadn't made it to the wedding, but she wished them the best.

"That's a blast from the past," said Dana, leaning against the kitchen counter. Like everything else in the house— including the white enamel electric range, the matching white refrigerator, and the yellow Formica counters. The next message continued to play.

"Hi, Pete." It was Mom. Pete tried not to roll his eyes. "I wasn't going to call until later, but your dad thought you should know right away. We just got a letter from Walt Freeman saying he thinks you're building on his land, and he says he's going to take all kinds of legal action if you don't fix it. Sorry for the bad news, but call as soon as you get back. Oh, and I hope you had a good honeymoon."

"What?" Dana's eyes widened, but Pete shook his head and sighed.

"He's confused," he told her. "My grandpa bought that land a long time ago. I have the paperwork."

"You're sure?"

"I'm sure. Look, don't worry. It's just a misunderstanding, OK? I'll take care of it."

She didn't look too sure, but the machine beeped again before playing one more message.

"Hi, Dana. Chad Duncan here." Dana's principal—her boss—could have been a radio announcer. "Say, I have something I need to talk to you about as soon as possible. Uh . . ." He paused before continuing. "Leslie's had to resign, uh, rather abruptly," he said. "Her last day was yesterday. I know this is very sudden, but we're going to need someone to fill in right away, on a temporary basis, and your name came up. So, uh, if you can call me, please do, and stop by my office first thing Monday and we'll talk, OK? See you then."

Pete watched Dana white-knuckle the edge of the counter.

"I thought Leslie was assistant principal," he said.

"She is—was."

"And they want you—?"

"Don't act so surprised."

His wife stood staring at the answering machine, starry–eyed.

"Was he joking?" Pete asked, trying for a bit of humor.

"I didn't think this would happen so soon," she said, ignoring his comment. "Who would have thought?"

"You mean you're just going to do whatever, just like that? Doesn't an assistant principal have to go to a lot more meetings and training and stuff?"

"It only sounds temporary to me. But you know, the pay is quite a bit better."

"Hmm, yeah. It just seems like a pretty big deal to just say, 'Sure, you bet.' The kind of thing we might want to think about maybe, you know?"

Dana stepped over and slipped her arms around his waist.

"I know. I didn't mean to imply we wouldn't. Besides, we have until Monday."

"Because for all they know, we could still be on our honey-moon, right?"

She planted a warm kiss on his lips and then looked at him with a smile.

"That's what I was hoping you'd say."

Chapter Three

How was Brownville?"

Charlotte stood in the door of the barn as she greeted her son. She didn't want to just jump at Pete with questions about Walt's letter. She would ease into it.

"Brownville?" Her son squinted up at her from where he sat on a tarp spread out next to the partially disassembled old tractor. "Yeah, we had a great time. I mean, you know. Dana did the antique shops. Lots of cool historic buildings. Nebraska's oldest river town, been there since 1854. She really liked it."

"And you did too?"

"Oh, sure." He wiped his brow with the back of his hand, still hefting a bracket of some sort that went with the broken starter. "But I can only take so many old clocks and wicker rocking chairs, you know."

"Well," she replied, smiling, "maybe I'll have to talk your father into taking me there sometime. You're back to work early, aren't you? Does your father know you're here?"

Pete shook his head and continued with his work.

"Haven't seen him yet. I think he's still out trying to plow the North Quarter. Must not be as wet as I thought."

Almost on cue, a tractor pulled up outside the barn and sputtered to a stop. Still, Pete continued wrestling with his project.

"Actually, Mom, I'm not really here. I was just going to drop this part by and get right back home. Dana's going to have dinner ready pretty soon."

Charlotte glanced at her watch. Four thirty. "This looks like a little more than just dropping a part by, don't you think?" she said.

"Yeah, well, I checked with Brad this afternoon, and the UPS guy came in the door with the part while we were on the phone. So I figured I'd grab it and run it over here, and then, heck, it should only take a few minutes to install. Can you hand me that bolt over there?"

Pete pointed with his chin so Charlotte could find what he needed. She moved her hand toward the parts scattered on the shelf.

"No, the other one."

Bob quietly stepped inside, located the bolt in question, and handed it over.

"This what you need?" he asked.

Pete looked up with surprise.

"Oh! I didn't hear you come in."

"Yeah, well, I did. You get your mom's message about Walt?"

Charlotte wished Bob would be a little more tactful, but she held her breath as Pete brushed off the question and returned to his work.

"Oh, that, yeah. Sorry I didn't get back to you. I got it under control."

Bob stood there with his hands on his hips, and Charlotte could tell he wasn't satisfied with his son's nonchalant answer.

"He's talking about legal—" Bob began, but Pete interrupted.

"I know, Dad. But really, it's no big deal. I'll take care of it."

Finally Bob shook his head with a curt "harrumph" and shrugged his shoulders. "It's your house; no skin off my nose. You just better deal with it."

"I will, OK?"

Pete didn't look at his dad, and Charlotte thought it best to change the subject.

"Well, maybe we should let him finish here," she told Bob. "I think I heard something about his new wife having dinner ready pretty soon."

Pete's grip slipped on his wrench, and he mumbled something about Dana running down to the school for a few minutes anyway.

"Oh well, in that case," said Charlotte.

"Reminds me," added Bob. "I'm hungry."

Pete tugged on his wrench once again.

"And I'll be done here pretty soon. Just a couple more minutes and I'll have this part bolted back in. Good as new."

Charlotte was pretty sure by the look of things and by the number of loose assorted parts scattered about that Pete was facing more than just a couple more minutes. "I'm going to run in and get that letter before you take off."

Perhaps there wasn't any real hurry to give him the letter, but still she scurried back across the gravel parking area and into her kitchen, glad the drizzle had tapered off. The phone was ringing as she stepped inside.

"Is someone answering that?" she yelled upstairs but got no reply. She snatched the receiver on the fifth ring.

"Hello, you've reached the Stevensons," came Bob's recorded voice. "We, uh, can't come to the phone right now, but if you . . ."

"I'm sorry!" Charlotte tried to catch her breath as she waited for the answering machine message to finish. When it finally did she was a little surprised to hear Jeff Santos, Sam's counselor at school. Jeff didn't sound quite so upbeat as he usually did.

"Actually, Mrs. Stevenson . . ." Jeff lowered his voice so Charlotte had to press her ear against the receiver to hear. "I've been trying to work with Sam about this, but he hasn't been cooperating much. So I thought you should know."

"Oh?" Charlotte wasn't sure what he meant, but it didn't sound good. "Is there a problem?"

Jeff sighed.

"All right, here's how it is." He sounded reluctant to explain. "I assume you know that in order to graduate, every student at Bedford High must complete a service project of their choosing."

Yes, Charlotte replied, she was aware of the requirement. Kids built park benches or volunteered at the convalescent home—that sort of thing. But that's about all she knew. The requirement had apparently been put into place after Pete's, Denise's, and Bill's high school days years ago. Now

Jeff went on to explain the details, as if Charlotte needed to know.

"There's the proposal, which we need to approve, the project itself, and a written report afterward. I'm the liaison, the contact person for all senior projects. That's why I'm calling, Mrs. Stevenson. Normally we get proposals nailed down by November or December—which would have been four months ago. Then the project takes place during the early part of the second semester, and final reports are turned in around March or April. Have you heard about any of this from Sam?"

"Honestly, no. We try to keep up with what he's doing, but lately he hasn't been sharing very much."

"That doesn't surprise me."

Charlotte paused. "I'm sorry. What are you saying, exactly?"

"I'm saying I haven't even received a proposal from Sam yet. And now with high school graduation in May, we're running out of time to get it done."

"I had no idea." Charlotte felt her face flush in embarrassment. She should have known. She should have asked more questions. "And you say he hasn't even—"

"He hasn't even told me what he's going to be doing. I've cornered him in the hallway once or twice, and all he will tell me is that he's working on it. He just seems to want to avoid the issue."

"Actually, that sounds like Sam."

"Maybe it does, but I can't twist his arm any more than I already have. I don't know if he understands the seriousness of this."

But Charlotte certainly did. No service project, no graduation.

"I'll speak with him right away, Jeff. Actually, I wish I'd known earlier, but . . ."

With a minimum of pleasantries they finished the conversation, and Charlotte hung up with a deep sigh. When she did, she noticed Christopher watching her from the kitchen doorway, nibbling on the corner of a graham cracker.

"Who was that, Grandma?" he asked.

"Never mind. Don't you have after-school chores to do? What about your lamb? Where's your brother?"

Christopher shrugged and pushed away from the wall.

"Dunno. He's not upstairs in his room. I haven't seen him for a while."

Charlotte peeked out the window to see if Sam's rusty little sports car was parked in its usual spot by the barn. It was.

"Are you sure you haven't seen him?" she asked.

"Not since we got home from school." He finished his graham cracker and stepped to the pantry for another. "Is he in trouble?"

"Not if I can help it," answered Charlotte, heading for the back door. She snapped up Walt Freeman's letter from the table, stuffed it in her sweater pocket, and headed back outside.

Sam was not out by the barn, and he was not by the horse corral. He was not in the fields or down by Heather Creek or anywhere else Charlotte could think to look. Pete hadn't seen him either, and his mechanical mess by the tractor was looking worse than before, if that were possible.

"Is it like some kind of emergency?" he asked. All she could see now were his legs poking out from under the engine. "Maybe you could call one of his friends."

Hmm. She considered it for a moment, until Emily walked by the barn with a bucket, probably on her way to check on the horses. Charlotte's granddaughter gripped a droopy umbrella as a token protection from the on-and-off rain, but still her blonde locks hung in the moist air. She would probably fix her hair with the blow dryer as soon as she got back inside.

"Christopher said you were looking for Sam," she told Charlotte matter-of-factly. She slowed down but didn't stop.

"Wait a minute." Charlotte caught up with her. "You know where he is?"

"Not exactly." Emily held her umbrella a bit higher. "I just know he went somewhere with Jake and Paul."

"And who was driving?"

"He didn't say. I didn't exactly see him leave."

"And he didn't say where they were going?" Charlotte wasn't sure how the boy could have slipped away without telling her or without her noticing. Perhaps while she was talking with Pete out in the barn?

"Nope. He just said he'd be back."

"Well, at least *you're* here."

"Not really. I'm staying over at Ashley's tonight, remember? She's going to pick me up in a couple of minutes."

"Oh. Did you tell me that earlier?"

Emily looked up at her grandmother as if to ask, "Is that

all?" before slipping away to do whatever it was she was going to do.

"And don't forget, Grandma." Emily paused just outside the door. "My birthday's coming up, and we're supposed to do a few more hours of driving so I can apply for my license."

"I haven't forgotten your birthday, and I haven't forgotten your driving."

Charlotte realized she might have sounded a little too cross, and she softened a little as Emily headed back to the house. "We'll do some more driving soon. If you're ever home, that is."

As Charlotte entered the barn, Pete found his way out from under the tractor; he grinned as he wiped his hands with a rag.

"What do you find that's so amusing?" she asked him.

"Nothing." He cleared his throat and watched Emily disappear into the house. "Just remember what I was like when I was her age. Not to mention Sam's age. It was worse then."

"I do have a vague recollection. Refresh my memory."

"Oh, come on. Cruising around when Dad wanted me to work. Disappearing all the time with my buddies. Looking for girls."

"Thanks for the reminder. I was hoping we had left that era behind."

"Mom, this is just the beginning. You know that. But he'll be OK. So will Emily. I mean, look at me: self-employed, honest grease on my hands, happily married. I survived."

"You survived, maybe. But you are not your nephew."

"True, I guess. But the point is, if I survived, anybody can."

"You could be right." She turned to go once more and then stopped to feel her pocket before pulling out the envelope. "Oh, I almost forgot. Here's Walt Freeman's letter."

Pete took the outstretched letter but frowned when he turned it over in his hand.

"Hmm, thanks," he told her, scanning the front of the envelope. "I guess."

Chapter Four

So, Paul, are they going to make you a captain or a general or what?" Jake Perkins stretched out in the front seat of Paul's old crew-cab pickup. Riding shotgun, he controlled the tunes. Right now they were playing U2 and some vintage rock.

Sam, being the "crew" on this aimless Friday evening ride about town, sat sideways across the little back seat, one knee scrunched up against Jake's seat. At least now that the rain had stopped they could roll down the windows again. It really wasn't that cold anyway. Paul Marshall, the square-jawed driver with the blond crew cut, snorted.

"Captain? Nah. I'd have to go to officers' school for that. First I've got to go to boot camp someplace—they've got like six boot camps—and then I get to choose some kind of training after that. I was thinking about being a Ranger."

"Cool." That apparently impressed Jake, who was probably all of 110 pounds and whose hair had a way of sticking up at all angles. "Those are the guys who fly into places with black face paint and do all the Rambo stuff, right? Maybe I should join the Rangers too."

The boys laughed. Everybody knew Jake would be going to UNL—the University of Nebraska at Lincoln. He would probably be delivering the valedictorian speech this year, maybe along with Melissa Sanchez, if she got a 4.0 GPA too. Plus he was definitely cleaning up on all the available scholarships to his college of choice. Not that he tried to, really. It just sort of happened that way for him.

"How many scholarships are they giving you, Jake?" Paul wanted to know. "You leaving any for anybody else?"

At first Jake looked as if he didn't want to answer, and he frowned at the question.

"Ah, I don't know. A couple."

"No, come on." Sam joined in. "It's not like it's some secret. I mean, everybody's going to hear about it at graduation when Mr. Duncan announces it."

Paul cupped a hand to his mouth and did a fair megaphone imitation of their principal.

"Jacob Perkins," he said, "winner of the studliest nerd award for this year."

"All right." Jake sighed as they circled the block and cruised down Lincoln Street once again. "There's the Rotary scholarship, the Nebraska rural schools scholarship, the Jennings and Beulah Haggarty scholarship, the Max and Margaret Pumphrey scholarship . . ."

"Hold it, hold it!" Paul interrupted this time. "You're not making this up, are you?"

"No, I'm not making this up. Would I make up names like Max and Margaret Pumphrey? It's a real scholarship, man. I didn't know anything about it until Mr. Santos told me. But hey, two thousand bucks is two thousand bucks. What can I say?"

The other boys considered that a moment, and Sam decided that no, he probably wasn't kidding.

"Sounds like they're paying you to go to school," said Paul, who probably should have been keeping his eyes on the road a little better. "But what about you, Sam? Did you ever get that soccer scholarship you were talking about?"

"Nah." Sam didn't want to get into all the details. They could talk about the other guys, but—

"Sam's going to go wherever his girlfriend goes," said Jake. "Right, Sam?"

Sam went along with that joke as best he could. It was better to keep things light than to get into the real story, which was for sure more boring than joining the Army Rangers or attending the U of N on a scholarship.

Leave it to Jake to raise the question and not leave it alone.

"Where are you going, really? I mean, you *are* going someplace, right? Like a college, I mean? You're not just working on your grandpa's farm, are you?"

"No! Are you kidding? No way. I would rather . . ."

His voice trailed off. He really wasn't sure what he would rather do, but he could say "no way" to the farm with absolute, unchecked certainty. No way would he be stuck on a farm for the rest of his life, like Uncle Pete. No way would he be feeding chickens and shoveling horse manure every day, every week, every month. Anything but that.

"Then what?" Paul wanted to know. "You going to get a job, like with computers, the way you said, or are you going to school?"

Sam shook his head and shrugged a shoulder, wishing they hadn't brought up the subject in the first place.

"Yeah," Jake joined in. "I haven't heard."

That's because there's nothing to hear, Sam wanted to say. Instead he just mumbled a noncommittal, "I'm still considering my options."

He guessed maybe they both knew what that meant, since it was already April and graduation was just over a month away. "I'm still considering my options" meant "I don't really have any options."

At least he was graduating, which was more than he could say for his Uncle Pete—though he would never dare bring that up in public.

On the other hand, the nagging thought occurred to Sam that he still had to get his stupid senior service project out of the way, and he couldn't think of any easy ways to keep Mr. Santos off his case. So he stared out the window, trying not to think about it, and as they passed Mel's Place for the third time his stomach growled.

"Dude, it's not like we were trying to bug you about it or anything." Jake sounded apologetic. "We were just asking."

"Yeah, no problem." Sam brushed it off. Really, it didn't matter to him one way or the other. "Look, how about we stop for a burger or something? I'm hungry."

The others had reasons why they couldn't stop. Paul didn't have any money and needed to get home soon. Jake had to study, or that's what he told them. Of anybody in the car, Jake most certainly did not need to study, especially on a Friday night.

"Fine." Sam gave up. "Maybe you'd better drop me off then too."

He meant at home, since that's where they'd picked him up. But they could have dropped him off anywhere. If they could have kept cruising all night, listening to U2 blaring on Paul's mediocre sound system, he would have done it. Anything to keep from going home.

"No hurry, I guess," said Paul, turning the music up even louder.

OK. For the next few minutes they drove around the block again and again, windows down, music loud, looking for other cars they knew, looking for girls they would like to know . . . just looking.

"Hey, isn't that your sister in Troy Vanderveen's truck?" Jake pointed down the block at someone just turning off on Bayard Lane.

"What?" That got Sam's attention, although he had only seen the tail end of the black Dodge pickup, and no one inside. "You're seeing things."

"No, I'm not," Jake insisted. "I'm like 94.2 percent sure that was her, and she was sitting pretty close."

"Did you see it, Paul?" Sam sat up straight and craned his neck, but the truck had disappeared. Paul shrugged.

"Maybe. I wasn't paying attention."

"Yeah, OK." Sam had to see if his little sister was really riding with Troy Vanderveen. Because if she was, he was going to have to sit her down and—

"Whoa." Jake thought it was funny. "Your sister's gone over to the dark side, huh? You think she's got a tattoo?"

"Knock it off, Jake." Sam cut him off and pointed down the block. "Follow the black truck, Paul. I've got to see if it's really her."

"Why don't you just call her and ask?" Jake put a hand up to his face, pretending it was a cell phone. "Hello, little sister? Are you making out with the school loser? Because if you are, my friends and I are going to come straighten you out."

Sam punched his so-called friend in the shoulder.

"Hurry up, Paul. Catch up to him!"

Chapter Five

K nock, knock." The principal's voice brought Dana out of the world of less-than-perfect term papers, and she looked up from the work left for her by the substitute teacher from the past week. How long had she been sitting there at her desk that afternoon, grading her students' efforts?

"Oh, hi. Come on in." She tried to sound as normal as she could, rather than as woozy as she felt. Too many term papers of questionable quality and creative use of grammar could do that to a person.

"What are you doing here? I didn't know you were back from your honeymoon already." Chad Duncan straightened his tie with his long fingers and stepped into her room, checking his watch as he did. "I was just finishing up with a short schoolboard meeting and noticed the light on here."

"Yep." She reshuffled the pile of papers on her desk. Surely he didn't want to hear the whole story. "Pete had a couple of jobs he needed to do at the farm, so I decided to come in and get a head start on next week."

Though it looked like an effort to do so, Mr. Duncan smiled, and then he pulled up a chair.

"I appreciate your dedication. I assume you got my phone message?"

"I did." She nodded. This meant they were getting straight to the point. "That was pretty unexpected news."

His face turned even more serious than his usual "all business" expression, and he stretched his long neck. Everything about Chad Duncan seemed long, from his size-12 tennis shoes to his face.

"It was a real blow to hear about Leslie, as you might guess. She's been a vital part of the team here for the past several years."

She nodded as he went on. Everyone liked Leslie Wellington. A little high-strung, but perhaps that came with working so closely with a man like Chad Duncan.

"And I feel for her with her family situation." Again he didn't explain. Dana supposed she would find out what had happened sooner or later. "But at this point that's neither here nor there. What the board and I discussed tonight was the need to plug in a qualified candidate for the remainder of the year, and then hopefully to put that person—or someone equally suitable—in place permanently as soon as possible. We want to hit the ground running when school resumes in the fall."

"That makes sense." Dana slipped her hands into her lap to keep them from shaking.

"The thing I told the board was that you already have a very good start on your master's in educational administration. Isn't that right?"

"I thought it was what I wanted to do at one point, but ..." She paused, trying to decide again how much he wanted to know. "But after a couple of semesters, honestly, I thought it would be best to remain in the classroom."

"And now?"

"Well, I'd certainly like to be considered. There aren't too many assistant principal spots this close to home, after all."

Again he smiled, and it seemed like a supreme effort.

"Good," he told her. "As long as you understand this is only a temporary assignment as we open up the interview process. We'll have to see if this is a good fit, and of course you're going to have some competition."

"Which means—"

"That means I'd like you to move your things into Leslie's old office as soon as possible. I'll walk you through a list of priorities for year's end, and I'll have you accompany me to a number of meetings. Here, may I show you a more detailed job description? I have a copy of it with me."

For the next forty-five minutes he went through a spiral-bound notebook with her, explaining a number of administrative duties as he turned the pages: textbook ordering, student class scheduling, working through the bus schedules, updating the custodial and cafeteria plans. Later there would be discipline and attendance oversight, counseling, safety plans, teacher evaluations, and more. Finally he paused and looked up at her.

"How does it look to you?" he asked.

Dana's head spun. It was one thing to hear over the phone that she might be considered for such an important position, even temporarily, but quite another to hear it in person from the principal himself. Frankly, it looked very much like a dream job to her.

"I . . . I say it all looks very good. I've always thought I'd like to really help shape the character of a school. But—"

She took a deep breath and put on her most professional demeanor.

Hold on, girl, she told herself. *Don't look too eager.* "But is it still all right if I talk it over with my husband a little more? We haven't really had a chance to discuss things since we got home."

"Yes, of course! I certainly didn't mean to rush you." Mr. Duncan got up from his chair. "And I really hadn't expected to be able to meet with you about this until after the weekend anyway. Like I said, I just noticed your light on and thought I'd take advantage of the opportunity. But of course, by all means discuss it with Pete. We'll touch base on Monday."

He stood and headed for the door as if he had somewhere to go and he'd suddenly realized he was late. But before stepping back out into the hall he rubbed his hands together and paused.

"I'm glad we were able to chat, Dana. And I'm hoping we can work together on this."

Dana didn't know how she could possibly turn down the opportunity, this shot at a dream job. And in her mind she had already decided to accept. Even so, she had also agreed with Pete that they would make these kinds of decisions together, that they would pray about it before saying yes or no.

Pete! By now he was surely sitting home alone, wondering what had happened to her. She left the papers on the desk, grabbed her purse, headed for the door, and turned out the lights.

TEN MINUTES LATER Dana stepped into the kitchen, hung her jacket carefully on the coat tree, and dropped her keys on the counter. She wished it were two hours earlier than the nine thirty showing on her little Betty Boop kitchen clock.

"I'm so sorry, honey," she told Pete, who sat at the table alone. "I was hoping to get home much earlier, but Mr. Duncan stopped by my room as I was finishing up grading papers, and he wanted to talk about the assistant principal thing. He's a little long-winded sometimes, you know."

"Yeah," he told her, taking another bite of the frozen pizza he had heated up. "No problem."

She picked up the pizza box and stuffed it into the garbage can under the sink. A candle in the middle of the table had burned most of the way down, spilling wax all over her cross-stitched doily, the one her Grandma Maxie had made. She would clean it up later.

"I feel bad," she said. "I was going to make you a nice dinner."

"I said no problem. You obviously had important stuff to talk about."

"Well, don't make it sound so horrible. You were the one who said you had to work this afternoon."

He glanced at his watch and stuffed the last of the pizza into his mouth. Had he really eaten the entire pizza?

"Yeah, but I made it a point to get home so we could have dinner, 'cause I thought that's what you wanted to do. I've been here a couple hours."

"Don't make me feel guilty. I told you it wasn't my fault."

"I know. Duncan wants to talk, so you gotta talk. Did he offer you the job?"

"Not permanently. I would just be filling in until they hire someone. But then I assume I might have a good chance. We'll see. I think he wants me to move into Leslie's office Monday."

"Hmm. More pay, huh? That'd help with the house."

"Which reminds me. What's up with that? Did you have a chance to talk to Walt Freeman or your parents about—"

"It's not a problem." He cut her off with a wave of his hand before she could really ask. "Like I told my folks, it's totally under control. So what did you tell Duncan anyway?"

Nothing like changing the subject. Pete obviously didn't care to talk about the house. What else could she say?

"I told him I'd discuss it with my husband."

He clamped his hands behind his head and leaned his chair back on two legs the way her most unruly students did. She gritted her teeth but held back what she wanted to say as he went on.

"Does this mean you're going to be coming home at nine thirty every night?"

"That will be before you make it home a lot of times."

"You think so?" He picked up a pizza crust and nibbled off the last sliver of burnt cheese. "Well, I'm used to frozen pizza. Guess that's the way it's going to be from now on."

Dana crossed her arms as she surveyed the mess on the table, the wrappers and dishes, and the pages of the *Bedford Leader* strewn around her kitchen. Was this really the way it was going to be? Not if she could help it.

"Here." She blew out the candle and picked up the waxy mess with the doily, hoping the heirloom might not be ruined. "At the very least, we're both going to need to keep things clean."

"Sure we are." He downed the dregs of a glass of milk and wiped his mouth with the back of his hand. It looked as if he had been working on some kind of engine and hadn't yet washed his hands. "I cleaned up some of the wedding-present wrapping paper tonight, plus I did a little decorating."

"Wait a minute. Decorating?" She looked around the little kitchen to see what he was talking about. Her cute yellow plaid curtains sill hung from the little window over the sink. The blue-and-white Danish plate from her Aunt Alice was still in its place on the wall. She would find a place for all her new things in their new house, but for now she had her little house decorated the way she liked. What was he talking about?

"It's nothing, really," he explained, motioning toward the compact living room and the front door. "Just my contribution to our unique home décor."

She held her breath as she peeked around the corner into the living room, hoping he hadn't hung something horrible on the wall like a tiki mask, a deer head, or a stuffed marlin. She gasped.

This was even worse.

"You're kidding, right?" she whispered. "Please tell me you're kidding."

"Would I kid you?" He rose to join her. "You know this is a collector's item. People would pay big bucks for this on eBay."

If only they would, thought Dana. She wondered what had happened to the nice framed Van Gogh *Vase with Daisies and Anemones* print she'd had there before. But naturally fine art couldn't compare to an ugly red-and-black movie poster of a grimacing man with a gun.

"He looks like he's in quite a lot of pain," she said.

"Who? Al Pacino? Nah. That's just the way he is in the movie. It's a classic. And it's guaranteed to be a great conversation starter, you know?"

"Yes," she said, walking over to the print. "But only one conversation—and we've just had it."

She carefully lifted the poster from the wall, walked over to Pete, and handed it to him.

"I'm sorry, honey," she told him, keeping her voice level. "But I just can't live with that horrible man staring at me like that. Not in this house and not in our new house either. If you want to put him up in the garage, that's up to you. I'd prefer you didn't, but I'm not going to stop you. I just guarantee you I'll never get within twenty feet of him."

"But . . ." He stared at Dana as if her reaction shocked him. "How can you not like Al Pacino? It's a classic."

Apparently that argument had been weighed on the scales and found wanting. She left him in the living room pondering his poster and returned to the kitchen to see if she could salvage her doily.

"I don't know about classics," she told him. "But I do think I'd like to take that job."

Chapter Six

Charlotte looked up at the mantel clock again, losing her place in her prairie romance novel one more time. It was nine—well before Sam's weekend curfew.

Meanwhile Bob snored over in his easy chair, soft and regular, even while he clutched the *Bedford Leader* on his chest. She thought of slipping it out of his grip and telling him to go to bed if he was going to sleep in his chair, but then she remembered the last time she'd tried that.

Better to leave hibernating bears alone.

When the phone rang out in the kitchen, Bob straightened and jerked upright with a snort and a confused look as the paper flew from his hand and fluttered in sections to the floor.

"What?" He looked at Charlotte. "What's that? Who's calling?"

Charlotte expected no good news from a nighttime call, particularly not this late.

The phone continued ringing.

"You want to answer it?" asked Bob. By now he had recovered a little clarity, although he still couldn't seem to get up out of the chair quickly enough.

"Not really." But she was already on her way into the kitchen. It rang yet again as she stood looking at the wall phone, dreading the bad news that surely awaited. Finally she took a deep breath and snatched the receiver off the hook, and indeed the woman caller sounded almost hoarse.

"It's Bev Davidson, dear, and I am so sorry to call this late."

"That's quite all right, Beverly. Is something wrong?"

"Well, I suppose you could call it that. Although I must tell you that no one appears hurt."

"Who, Beverly? Who doesn't appear hurt?"

That got Bob's attention, and he quickly appeared at the kitchen doorway with an even more puzzled expression on his face.

"Let me tell you." Bev sounded as if she were hyperventilating. "It's just not every day the police pull someone over in front of my house. Right there in front! For a moment I thought they were going to pull straight into the rose bushes! And after all the pruning I did this spring, that would have been a crying shame. You know I've had those rose bushes for going on twenty-two years. My husband's mother gave them to us as a wedding present, and that would have been—"

"Here, let me have this thing." Bob took the receiver and pressed it to his ear.

"Bev!" He nearly barked into the phone. "What's happening over there?"

After that, Bob just listened and nodded, interjecting the occasional "uh-huh" and "I understand."

"You sure it was him?" he finally asked. "And he wasn't driving?"

"Is Sam OK?" whispered Charlotte, but Bob just shook his head and ignored her.

I should have held on to the phone, she thought as Bob finally thanked Beverly before he hung up.

"Well?" asked Charlotte. Bob crossed his arms and frowned at her.

"Bev says your grandson was in a pickup that was stopped by the police right in front of her house in town. She thought we should know."

"Thought we should know? What happened? Who else was in the car? Were they OK? Could Bev tell if there was any drinking involved?"

"Hold it, hold it." He held up his hands. "All I know is what she told me."

"Who was driving?"

"Bev says she couldn't tell exactly what was going on with her binoculars, but she didn't see any signs of booze."

"But who was driving, Bob?"

"Paul Marshall."

She groaned as Bob finished relaying Bev's report.

"Jake Perkins was in the passenger seat, with Sam behind him."

"And Bev didn't know why the boys were stopped?"

"Well, from what she heard out the window, apparently Jake told the officer they were following Troy Vanderveen and Emily."

"Wait. Troy who? Was she sure? Emily is spending the night at Ashley's house."

"Well, I wouldn't trust what Bev says Jake says he thinks he saw."

"I wouldn't either."

Charlotte could just imagine Beverly Davidson crouching behind the curtains in her living room, poking her field glasses out through her curtains and listening out the window to what was going on. It was almost comical. And the way the Bedford rumor mill worked, Charlotte expected they'd have more details—accurate or otherwise—in just a few minutes.

The question was, what had Sam and the other boys in that pickup done to get themselves into trouble that way?

"They were probably speeding," said Bob, returning to the living room. "Either that, or Paul ran a stop sign or some fool thing. We'll have a talk when Sam gets back."

Charlotte heard the gentle thump of footsteps on the stairs.

"Who called?" Christopher wanted to know. This eavesdropping on phone conversations was getting to be a pattern, wasn't it? He crouched halfway down the stairs, gripped the banister, and stared down at them.

"You get on back to bed, pal." Bob didn't answer him directly. "You're going to wake up your sister."

"She's not here, remember?"

"I knew that." Bob wrinkled his forehead, as if he had just remembered again where Emily was spending the night.

"But who was speeding?" Christopher persisted. "Was Sam speeding? Is he in trouble?"

"No, Sam was not speeding." Now Charlotte joined the exchange. "And the only person in trouble right now is you if you don't get back to bed."

Christopher backed up slowly, one step at a time.

"I'm worried about Magic."

Now it was Charlotte's turn to be confused.

"Magic?" she asked. "Who or what is magic?"

Bob and Christopher exchanged a knowing look.

"Tell her, Grandpa."

"You tell her. It's your lamb."

"Well, OK." Christopher looked pleased at the brief reprieve, and he sat down on the nearest step. "See, after the lamb got away from us the other day, Grandpa said he disappeared like magic, and I thought it was a cool name. So we named the lamb Magic."

"Hmm. I've never heard of a lamb named Magic." Charlotte knew a delaying tactic when she heard one, but just then she heard the soft click of the back door, which meant Sam must have arrived home.

"All right." She waved at Christopher to shoo him upstairs. "That's enough about Magic for now."

"But I'm worried about him," countered Christopher. "He's not as playful as I thought he was going to be. He just runs away. The book about sheep I got says that—"

"You can tell us later." She wished Bob would play the "bad guy" part right now, but he didn't step in. "It's too late to be worrying about Magic. He's probably just tired and a little scared. You know what it's like to leave your home and go to a new farm. We'll see how he is in the morning, all right?"

"All right." He finally agreed, pointing just over her shoulder. "It looks like Sam is home."

With that he turned and ran back up the stairs, as if expecting fireworks. And as a matter of fact, Sam did try to slip by Charlotte and Bob on his way to the stairs. Thankfully Bob managed to block him just in time.

"Hang on there, buddy," Bob told him. "I think we need to have a little chat."

Sam looked surprised, even though he shouldn't have. His shoulders slumped when Bob nodded toward the kitchen and told him to have a seat.

"We just got a phone call from Mrs. Davidson," Bob started in.

Sam groaned. "Who?"

"Mrs. Davidson. She lives in the house where you were pulled over."

"Oh."

"You want to tell us?" asked Charlotte.

"I should have guessed," he answered with a frown. "The gossip patrol in action. I'll bet she already called Paul's mom too, huh? Gave her the whole scoop?"

"We're not talking about Paul's mom," said Charlotte, although he had probably guessed correctly. "We're just concerned about you. And we—"

"What was Paul doing?" Bob interrupted with the intensity of a prosecutor as he paced around the kitchen table. He could have softened up just a little. "Was he speeding?"

Charlotte wasn't surprised that Sam stiffened and recoiled. She might have done the same if she'd been in his position.

"We were just driving around, hanging out. I had no

idea Paul was speeding until we got pulled over. None of us did. Not even Paul. And even then, I think he was probably only going thirty-five or forty at the most."

"In the neighborhood. No wonder he was pulled over."

"Grandpa—"

"No, you listen here." By this time Bob had heated up, and he was wagging his finger pretty well. Charlotte cringed at the sight, although she understood her husband's frustration. Why so much arguing lately? Sam just stuck out his chin and clamped his lips together.

"If you want to graduate from high school you're going to have to keep your nose clean, do you understand?"

Sam nodded, but his expression steeled even more as he crossed his arms and his grandfather continued.

"That means staying out of vehicles where the driver's going to be clowning around. That means not riding with Paul Marshall anymore. And that means using a little judgment, for crying out loud."

"Who says I'm going to graduate?" asked Sam. It wasn't entirely clear that he was serious. Surely he couldn't be.

"Of course you're going to graduate, Sam." Charlotte told him, trying to cool down the confrontation a bit. "Please don't even say that. Although I should mention I got a call from Mr. Santos, and he was quite concerned that you hadn't completed any part of your senior service project yet. Do you want us to help you come up with ideas?"

Instantly she regretted pouring that kind of fuel on this fire—but she had promised to bring it up, hadn't she? Red-faced, Sam pushed back his chair and got to his feet.

"What is it with this place? Mrs. What's-her-name calls you with a gossip report. What was she, peeking through the shades with her spyglass? And Mr. Santos calls you about that stupid service project thing? I can't believe it."

"Sam—" Charlotte began, but changed her mind. Bob opened his mouth as if to object too, but she shook her head at him. For now they would let Sam vent.

"Well, the speeding ticket wasn't my fault," Sam told them, "so you can both relax about that. I wasn't driving, OK? And the service project is under control, so you and Mr. Santos don't need to keep ragging on me about it. I don't need any help."

"Sam," said Bob, "I don't think anybody is ragging on you about anything."

"Well, I don't need the homework police on my case; that's all." He headed for the stairs again, and this time they let him go. But he paused at the door. "Oh, and by the way, is Emily home tonight?"

"She's spending the night at Ashley's," answered Charlotte. And as far as she knew, that was the truth of it—despite what anyone had seen or not seen.

He stood there a moment, fists clenched, as if trying to decide something. She was about to ask him if there was anything else when he just grunted and stormed away.

Charlotte squeezed her eyes, praying she had said the right thing and begging God for wisdom to deal with a teen boy she didn't understand. She'd probably said too much. But when she opened her eyes again, Bob was still staring at her, hands on his hips and looking less than pleased.

"I still don't think we're getting through to that kid," he said.

For Sam's sake, she hoped her husband was wrong.

Chapter
Seven

B y the time the following Tuesday rolled around, Charlotte was surprised at how much progress was being made on Pete's house. Permits, plans, foundations—Pete certainly wasn't wasting any time getting started on the modest little house he had planned on the far corner of their property, over on the rise bordering the Freemans' acreage.

Charlotte was worried about Walt Freeman's objections. Had Pete and Walt really settled the dispute so quickly?

She hoped so. It was such a pretty spot, with a striking view over their fields and a well-used tractor trail already carved along the fence line as a driveway. No doubt about it: Pete and Dana had picked a beautiful site for their new home.

As Charlotte cleaned up after lunch she thought perhaps Pete and his workers could use a little refreshment.

She loaded a basket with jam-filled muffins and added some paper cups with the thermos of steaming black coffee. Even if April had warmed up a few degrees, she imagined they'd still like a cup of afternoon coffee.

She listened for the rumble of trucks and the shout of workers as she stepped out the back door with her load of snacks, but heard nothing. Perhaps they were taking a break. She walked through the field and up the gravel road to the building site.

They're being awfully quiet, she told herself. *Much quieter than I expected.*

When she arrived at the site a big delivery truck was parked off to the side, idling beside a large stack of lumber that had been unloaded. Several other pickups were parked on the fringes of the work zone.

Instead of busying themselves with a thousand projects they probably could have been doing, the four carpenters had gathered in a semicircle around Pete, who stood next to a scattered maze of two-by-six framework with his hands on his hips, obviously in a deep discussion with their neighbor, Walt Freeman.

Nobody seemed to notice Charlotte walking up with her snacks, and she hesitated a moment, feeling out of place. Walt was very animated, waving some kind of large paper —maybe a set of blueprints or an unfolded roadmap—and jabbing at it with his free hand.

"I'm telling you, it's right here," Walt told Pete. Without a hat, wisps of thin silver hair stuck up every which way, making him look like a wild professor delivering a lecture. "That's what I was trying to explain in my letter. The one you ignored."

"I didn't ignore it," replied Pete. "I just didn't think—"

"Yeah, that's your problem, Pete. If you had asked me before you went and did all this work, I could have saved you a lot of money and a lot of trouble. Could have saved all of us a lot of trouble. Wish I'd taken the time to look a little closer right from the start, but that's not my responsibility, is it? And now you're going to have to rip everything up."

"Hold on, Walt." Pete obviously wasn't backing down. "I know you think your property line runs through here, but—"

"Right through that corner." Walt made a chopping motion over the corner of the foundation. "According to my map, you've encroached at least twenty feet."

"That's according to your map," replied Pete. "And how old is it?"

"Doesn't matter how old it is. In fact, the older the better. Shows what really is."

"Walt!" Pete leaned over for a closer look. "That thing is from 1932. You're not telling me you're still working with a map that's as old as you are."

"Just for the record, I'm not quite that old. Fact is, this map proves what I'm trying to tell you. It proves you're encroaching."

"See, that's not what I understand, and that's not what the surveyor I was working with told me. We have the edge of your property fifty feet over that way." He pointed toward a small cluster of oaks. "We might be a little close, but there's no way we're on your property."

All this time the workers were watching the back-and-forth between the two men the same way they might watch a tennis match. Back and forth, and then again. And still Charlotte wasn't sure this was the right time to interrupt. But she was getting tired of holding her basket of muffins, so she waded into the fray.

"Excuse me, gentlemen." She set her basket down on another pile of lumber, this one of neatly stacked two-by-fours. "I thought perhaps you could all use a little midafternoon refreshment. Some muffins and coffee? How about you, Walt?"

Walt shook his head. "No thanks, Charlotte. I need to get going."

"Walt, wait a minute." Pete held out his hand. "We still need to resolve this."

"Oh, it's resolved, as far as I'm concerned." Walt folded up his map. "You're building part of your house on my land, period. Look, I'm sorry you went to all this trouble. But you go ask at the county planning office; they'll tell you the same thing I'm trying to tell you. You've got to pull it back off the line."

Charlotte looked around at the work already done—the foundation and the steps, the outline of the walls. She could imagine a cute little place here, with several clusters of mature oaks providing shade against the summer heat, maybe a lawn in front where little grandchildren could play.

"You don't think you could compromise on a couple of feet?" she asked. Neither man seemed to hear her.

"Listen, Walt," said Pete. "I'll be sure to go to the planning office all right. You know I don't want to do anything out of line. But honestly I think you're going to be surprised at what they tell us. When you're working with an outdated survey . . ."

"Humph." Walt turned his head and spit. "Nothing out-dated about the line between you and us. It's the same now as it was back in '32."

Charlotte started to pour a steaming cup of coffee. Blessed are the peacemakers, right?

"You sure you won't have a cup, Walt? I made it extra-strong, just the way you like it. And really, it sounds as if we can come to some kind of a compromise here."

"Compromise?" Walt shook his head once again as he broke away from the group. "We're talking about some-one building his house on my property. You wouldn't like someone else doing that on your property, would you?"

"Mom, you don't know what this is all about." Pete didn't seem to appreciate her perspective either.

"I'm sorry." Charlotte pulled back. She hadn't meant to interfere. And now Walt pointed at Pete, as if to warn him.

"Any work you do here is going to be wasted; you know that."

"I don't know anything of the sort." Pete turned to the other men. "In fact, these fellows here are going to keep right on framing."

Pete could be quite stubborn when he wanted to be. Dig-in-his-heels stubborn, just like his dad.

"Let's go." Pete clapped his hands. "We've got a lot of work to do, and we've already lost too much time standing around here yakking. Thanks for stopping by, Walt. We'll be in touch."

The other men looked at each other with raised eye-brows but did as they were told. Walt nodded and stuffed his map under his arm before doing an about-face and marching over to his truck. So much for a neighborly discussion. That left Charlotte standing there with her muffins and coffee.

"Pete," she said, lowering her voice. "Are you sure you know what you're doing? Shouldn't you ask your father?"

"Already discussed it with him once," he replied, holding out a cup for her to pour him some coffee. "Months ago, after the fire, when we first decided to put a house here."

"What about Walt's map?"

Pete took a sip of the coffee and reached for a muffin. At least someone appreciated them.

"Walt's mixed up. He's got this ancient map and thinks he knows everything. The surveyor I worked with told me we should be fine."

"All right, but you're still going to make sure everything is OK with the planning office, won't you? You need to settle this with the Freemans in a good way. They've been our neighbors for many years, you know."

"Mom, would you relax? Everything's under control."

"You sound just like Sam."

"What?"

"Never mind."

"YOU SHOULD HAVE STAYED out of it," Bob told her later after he came in for a break from plowing the North Quarter and she was putting together a salad for dinner later.

"Yes, I know," she admitted, chopping the lettuce and

tomatoes. "But all I was doing was bringing them some muffins and coffee, and—"

"And you probably got on Walt's bad side."

"How could I get on his bad side?" Charlotte asked. "I was just bringing the boys some muffins and coffee."

"You mentioned that. But this is Pete and Dana's place, so Pete and Dana are going to have to figure it out for themselves." He held up his hands. "We have to be hands off, and we've got to keep our mouths shut."

"Even if it's our land?"

"It's going to be properly deeded over to them. But yes, even if it's our land."

"And even if it's our neighbors?"

When he looked at her sideways, she knew the answer to her own question.

"All right." She pulled a bunch of carrots out of the refrigerator and started cutting those as well. "I will try not to interfere. But I do not want this to turn into a feud where we're caught in the middle, and—"

"Charlotte! There's not going to be any feud."

She returned to her cooking as Christopher joined them in the kitchen, looking forlorn. This time she welcomed the chance to change the subject.

"How's Magic doing?" she asked. "Does he seem happier now?"

"Not so sure." He leaned up close to her, as if inspecting her cooking. "I think you need to come check with me again."

"What about Emily? Maybe she could go with you."

"Emily's never around anymore. She's always off with her friends."

"And Sam?"

"He's with Paul or Jake. He's always with those guys."

"What about some of your friends? Can't you invite them over? I haven't seen Dylan for a while."

"Dylan's been sick."

For a brief moment it almost looked as if Christopher were about to cry, but then he wiped the back of his hand across his face and sniffed. Charlotte bent over and looked at him a little closer.

"Are you all right, Christopher?" she asked. "You look a little down."

"I just think we need to check on Magic, that's all. I don't want him to get sick too."

Charlotte nodded, but she still wasn't sure. She couldn't remember seeing Christopher quite this clingy or this depressed.

Something else had to be wrong.

Chapter Eight

That Friday evening Sam was thrilled to be going to the movies in Harding with Arielle. It didn't matter to him what movie they were seeing, just that she had agreed to go with him. He hoped that meant they were back together. The night would be perfect as long as she didn't start asking about his senior project or about graduating. Anything but that.

He passed a ten across the snack counter for some popcorn and a couple of sodas. Medium Diet Coke for Arielle, monster-sized regular Coke for him.

"You know artificial sweetener rots your brain," he told Arielle. He was relieved when she returned his grin.

"You know high-fructose corn syrup rots your teeth," she quipped back at him, flipping a lock of her pretty raven hair out of her eyes.

"Hmm," he said, taking their bucket of popcorn and the meager change. "Rotten teeth or rotten brain. I know which one I'd pick. Of course, you have a lot more brain to spare."

"Stop it." She elbowed him in a nice sort of way as they headed for the best seats in the house—five rows back, center.

A few minutes later as they sat waiting for the previews, he ran out of things to say, and Arielle must have taken that as a sign that something was wrong.

"You OK?" she asked, eating one delicate piece of popcorn at a time. He pointed to his full mouth, and she waited patiently as he finished chewing.

"Sure." He kind of choked.

Sometimes it felt as if Arielle could take one look at him and guess exactly what was going on in his head.

"You're still worried about the other night?" she asked, further proof that she could read minds. "I hope you told your grandparents it wasn't your fault. Paul's the crazy driver, not you."

That was true most of the time.

"Grandma knows." He took a sip of his soda to wash down the popcorn. "They don't like me riding with Paul. But they know it wasn't my fault."

"Then what?" She was going to find out sooner or later. He just needed to steer the conversation clear of his senior service project. He parked his drink on the floor by his feet.

"OK," he said. "Here's the part I didn't tell you yet."

She lifted her eyebrows.

"See," he went on, "the reason Paul was speeding the other night was because I was telling him to."

"What? Why would you do that?" She leaned a little closer.

"I was just telling him to catch up to Troy Vanderveen's truck, 'cause I saw my little sister sitting in the front seat with the guy."

"You mean Emily was—"

"Yeah. And the thing is, she was supposed to be staying overnight at Ashley's house. So I don't know if she was on her way to Ashley's, or out cruising, or what. Either way, it's not good, and I don't like it."

"Hmm. You didn't say anything to your grandparents about that, did you?"

"Are you kidding? They would freak out, even if Troy is the neighbor's . . . what is he to the neighbor guy, a nephew?"

"Mrs. Freeman's sister's son. Right. A nephew."

Sam shook his head. "I'm still blown away by how many people are related around here. Everybody at school is cousins or second cousins, I mean . . . not you."

"That's nothing," she told him with a mischievous little grin. She looked around, as if to make sure her relatives weren't in the theater. "Did I ever tell you how Lisa MacDonald went to prom with this guy, and it wasn't until the slow dances they figured out they were related? They were distant cousins, only they didn't even know it."

"Eeew." Sam wrinkled his nose. "What if they had started kissing or something? There's gotta be a law against that. One more reason to get out of Bedford ASAP."

This time she didn't pop right back with a silly answer, the way he would have expected. Instead she just kind of sat there, staring at the ads that came up on the screen, as if she really needed to pay attention. She stayed quiet through all the previews too. Not a word.

"Just kidding about Bedford." Sam wondered if he had just inserted foot in mouth since he was talking to the girl whose family had been living in the town her whole life. "I didn't say anything wrong, did I?"

But when she finally turned to him her eyes looked big and kind of scared, and he had no idea what had brought that on.

"I got accepted at another college," she told him, "and I'm really thinking of going there."

"Where?"

"Well, I was waiting for the right time to tell you. But maybe there's no right time."

Except maybe now, while a preview came on for some super-lame English movie in a garden and the people had funky white wigs on, which he didn't mind ignoring.

"That's good news, isn't it? Unless it's far away. I mean . . ." He felt that foot in his mouth once again. "No, really, I mean, whatever *you* think is best, *I* think is best too."

She smiled at that, but not the kind of smile that made his heart flutter. The colored light from the movie screen made her face look weird.

"It's a Christian college in Minnesota."

He nodded his head and tried to look like whatever she'd said was fine with him when it really wasn't. Wow. Did she know how far away Minnesota was?

"Oh . . . that's cool." He forced out the words and swallowed hard. "What was the big deal about telling me?"

They both knew the big deal. The big deal was that going to school far away meant she wouldn't be close to home, and not being close to home meant not being close to him. And maybe she would meet some other guy at this school who was studying to be a preacher or a missionary.

Minnesota. Sam wasn't sure what to feel. After all, he and Arielle had just started dating again and he really wasn't sure where things were headed. He had hoped they would continue seeing each other, but they had no real commitment. She was free to go to college wherever she wanted.

He had to admit she looked a little conflicted as well. But heck, it was her decision, so she could always decide on another college if she wanted to. It's not like she hadn't been accepted by enough other schools. A few of them were even pretty close to home.

"But you're not sure yet?" He just thought he'd ask.

"I'm still thinking about it."

What more could he ask? The theater was darkening for the main feature, and Sam supposed he and Arielle had probably said everything they had to say—about Paul's driving, about Emily and Troy, and about Sam and Arielle.

"OH, I DON'T KNOW." Ashley's voice sounded far away, like her cell phone didn't have good coverage. "I really wouldn't want to say anything bad about him. But ..."

"But what?" Emily squeezed her eyes shut as she sprawled on her bed. She kept her voice down so nosy Christopher wouldn't overhear her through the closed door. Or nosy Grandma.

"I shouldn't say, Emily."

"Well, I'm sure it's not true anyway. People say lots of bad things about Troy that aren't true."

Ashley paused just long enough to cast a shadow on the conversation.

"Come on," Emily finally said. "Tell me."

"Well, OK. You know his friends got kicked out of school for spray-painting graffiti on the play equipment at the park."

"His friends, but not him. And he doesn't hang out with those guys much anymore."

"Well..." Ashley caught her breath for a moment. "Nobody ever proved anything. But I heard he was there too. And there was a bunch of shoplifting last year in Harding they thought—"

"Troy would never do that sort of thing."

"See? That's what I mean, Emily. I know you like him, so I don't want to say anything bad. But you do know he smokes, right?"

"Have you ever actually seen him smoke?"

"Well, no. But sometimes you can smell the smoke when he walks by in the hall. It's gross."

This time it was Emily's turn to pause. Yeah, she knew. But all the other stuff—the vandalism, the shoplifting, getting suspended—those were things the other guys did, not Troy.

"Emily? Are you sure you want me to..." Ashley sounded really far away now, and her voice faded in midsentence. Emily checked her phone, and once again it had dropped a call.

She sighed. Other people didn't understand how nice Troy really was. He was different.

Wasn't he?

Chapter Nine

Early Monday morning Pete sat on his tailgate next to the job site of his new home, breathing in the fresh scent of dew from the fields and watching the early morning sun creep over the horizon. A symphony of birds surrounded the framing on his house project, which had attracted a pair of robins who were looking as if they thought building a nest there would be a splendid idea.

"Sorry, guys." He waved at the noisy pair as if that would do any good. They fluttered away to watch him suspiciously from the branches of a young oak a few yards away. The workers would be arriving in a half hour.

Meanwhile Pete opened the worn little pocket Bible he carried in the glove box of his truck and leafed through the pages randomly. Sometimes he felt guilty for not following along in the "Bible in a year" plans Pastor Evans wanted them to follow. He'd done that once and had felt quite proud of himself for doing so. This year, he'd taken to catching a chapter or a verse here and there. Maybe he just had three too many things on his mind.

Number one, naturally, was being married, which he had originally thought was going to be a fairly simple matter but which now seemed to be anything but. Number two was the farm. It was time for spring planting, and even if Dad was raring to go, he wasn't. Pete was continually frustrated by working with him, yet he couldn't deny that he needed the help.

Number three was right in front of him—the new house and the numerous details that came with building it. Permits, plans, blueprints, framers, electricians, concrete guys, materials lists. Who knew that being one's own contractor meant making so many decisions?

On top of all that, he had to keep Dana happy and his dad happy and everyone else in Bedford happy while keeping the farm afloat too. Oh, and the whole border dispute thing with Walt Freeman, which didn't seem to be going away. Was that more than three things?

This is giving me a headache just thinking about it, God.

He sighed and tried to pray as he flipped through a few more pages, wishing God would answer back and tell him how to get through all the new headaches that had piled on him just in the past couple of weeks. He tried his favorite "needle-in-the-haystack word-from-God" technique of rifling through the pages, closing his eyes, and landing a finger on the divine "answer."

"Sorry, God," he prayed. "I know this is theologically iffy, but I really need to know."

His initial attempt landed him on the first chapter of 1 Chronicles in the Old Testament. "The sons of Ham," he read. "Cush, Mizraim, Put and Canaan. The sons of Cush: Seba, Havilah, Sabta, Raamah and Sabteca."

That passage wasn't helpful at all, and he couldn't see what it had to do with balancing his out-of-control life. So he tried again, happening upon a passage in the book of Acts: "They had such a sharp disagreement that they parted company. Barnabas took Mark and sailed for Cyprus...."

"*Hmm.*" He frowned. "Reminds me of what's going on with my neighbor."

He wasn't feeling inspired yet, and though he was pretty sure Pastor Evans would not approve, he tried yet again to find a passage that spoke to him. Finally he came upon another Old Testament passage, one from the prophet Jeremiah: "If you stay in this land," he read, "I will build you up and not tear you down; I will plant you and not uproot you."

Jackpot! Finally something he could relate to, even though it had originally been written by a long-ago prophet. He read on.

"Do not be afraid of the king of Babylon, whom you now fear. Do not be afraid of him, declares the LORD, for I am with you and will save you and deliver you from his hands. I will show you compassion so that he will have compassion on you and restore you to your land."

He wasn't so sure about the king of Babylon, but if he could plug Walt Freeman into that role, this section of the scriptures potentially made a whole lot of sense. Hanging on to their land would be a good thing, just like it was a good thing for the Israelites, right?

A truck came rumbling up the lane, interrupting his theological wonderings. Looked like the supplier from A-1 Lumberyard, loaded down with more framing timbers.

"Hot dog." Pete set his Bible aside and rose to meet the delivery. "Right on time."

That was the good news. The not-so-good news came just a few minutes later, after the young driver had dumped his load of lumber and handed Pete the invoice. Pete took one look and nearly fainted.

"Hold it—whoa, whoa, whoa." Pete held it up for the driver to see. "This isn't what John quoted me a few weeks ago. Not even close."

The kid shrugged his shoulders.

"Sorry. I don't have anything to do with the pricing. I just deliver the stuff."

"But wait a minute." Now Pete had a chance to do a little figuring. "You guys jacked your prices up like twenty, twenty-five percent since I last saw them."

Again the delivery guy shrugged, but he was moving back to the cab of his big flatbed truck and clearly didn't want to talk lumber prices with Pete.

"Like I said, I just—"

"Yeah, I know. You just deliver the stuff."

"Do you want me to take it back?"

He wasn't serious, and Pete knew any other lumberyard would probably charge even more. Even so, he didn't like the feeling of suddenly being out an extra five hundred dollars, just like that. With five hundred dollars he and Dana could take a nice vacation or buy one of those cool stainless steel deluxe outdoor grills he'd seen on those TV home shows. The driver interrupted his thoughts.

"I mean, I can load it all up on the truck again, if that's what you want." This kid came with an attitude all right.

"No, no." Pete waved him off. He wasn't trying to be

rude. "Just tell John to give me a call. There's some kind of mistake here."

"Whatever." The young guy climbed back into his cab and started the engine with a roar, leaving Pete in a sooty cloud of diesel smoke.

Is this the compassion I was just reading about? Pete asked God, though he admitted it didn't sound quite as respectful as it probably should have. He remembered the passage he'd just read: *I will show you compassion so that he will have compassion on you and restore you to your land.*

Nice idea, but . . . His cell phone rang and he quickly checked the number before snapping it open.

"What's up, Mom?" He tried not to sound impatient with her, but this really wasn't a good time.

"Oh, hi." She sounded far away rather than just across the field. "I can't believe you actually picked up," she said, a bit surprised.

"Well, Dana insisted I get this thing, so I'm trying to get used to it," Pete replied.

"I was just wondering what happened at the planning office last week," Charlotte continued. "You did go, didn't you?"

He nodded his head, but realized she couldn't see him.

"Yes, I went, Mom."

"What did they tell you?"

"Nothing I didn't already know."

"Which means?"

"Which means they don't know for sure what Walt is talking about, but they're going to look into it and get back to me."

"Oh." She paused. "Maybe you should ask your brother

to help with this. He's very good at figuring out this kind of thing."

"No, Mom. I'm sure Bill has enough to do. And besides, I don't think it would look good to have the mayor of another town checking into this."

"Well, I don't think it would be a prob—"

"It's all good, Mom. We'll get it figured out. Meanwhile, I've got framers showing up here any minute."

"All right then. I didn't mean to interfere. We were just wondering. Say hi to Dana for me."

He said good-bye and snapped his phone shut, trying to avoid the thought in the back of his mind that he probably didn't need to be so rude to his mother.

He really wished everyone would relax about the property. The work was moving ahead despite Walt's challenge. Pete was sure they would get everything figured out soon, and to their advantage. No way could he have encroached on the neighbor's property. Absolutely no way.

He checked his watch before climbing up into the back of his truck for a better view toward the road. Seven thirty.

"What's keeping those guys?" he mumbled to himself. They had promised to get here no later than seven fifteen. He stood watch for another ten minutes, arms crossed, pacing around the bed of his truck and ignoring the rest of the glorious morning.

"Come *on!*" He kicked at the truck tire in frustration. He had to get these guys working, and then he would run over to help Dad with some tractor work in the North Quarter.

His cell phone rang, and he flipped it open once more, starting to get annoyed by these interruptions.

"Yeah?" he snapped. No "good morning" nonsense when it wasn't.

"Hey, boss." Nick the framer sounded more upbeat than he had a right to. "We're having some car troubles here, so Randy had to go borrow his brother-in-law's wheels. Be there in a half hour. Just wanted you to know, OK?"

"Not OK." Pete made a fist and clenched his teeth. "I'm standing here waiting, and nothing is getting done."

"Sorry, boss. Nothing I can do about it. We'll be there real quick."

"Yeah, you be here real quick."

Pete snapped his phone shut again with a frown. The heat in his cheeks reminded him of the argument with Dana the other night about the classic but stupid Al Pacino poster. He hopped down off the back of the truck and walked over to where the framed outline of the large garage stood, where Dana had mentioned he might consider hanging the poster.

Funny how a little thing like that could make or break an evening. Just like now, when a little thing like his workers being late could send him into a tizzy. He caught his breath.

I will show you compassion so that he will have compassion on you and restore you to your land.

The words rang in his ears.

What's wrong with me?

He wasn't sure, but he knew he didn't like it. Even worse, he knew he didn't like the way it had put a wedge between him and Dana . . . the way he knew it should not have.

Before he could talk himself out of it, he pulled out his cell phone again and punched in the school number. The receptionist answered with a chirpy "Good morning, Bedford High School. How may I direct your call?"

This time he lost the surly voice.

"Hey, good morning, Margo, it's Pete Stevenson. Is Dana there?"

He could almost hear the smile on the other end of the line.

"You mean your wife?" She might have giggled. "Actually, she's in a meeting with Principal Duncan. Do you want me to put you through to her voice mail?"

"Yeah, I mean . . ." He thought for a moment how lame an apology would sound on her voice mail, but persisted. "Actually, fine, sure. I'll talk to her machine."

After the beep he gave her his humble version of "I'm sorry I was a jerk the other night," complete with his promise to keep Al Pacino out in the garage.

"I guess you're busy gearing up for that new job," he added, "but I just want you to know I'll support whatever you want to do. Love you."

He hung up, hoping he'd said the right thing this time. Maybe they could have lunch if she wasn't still busy.

Chapter Ten

I'll make up a list of textbooks we ordered last year." Mr. Duncan never stopped talking as they wove through the halls on their way to the teaching conference room. "But that's just a template. So I'll need you to personally check with every teacher before the last day of class to confirm titles and numbers."

"Titles and numbers, check." Dana scribbled in her notebook and tried not to step on his heels as she followed behind. She hoped her hair was holding up and her appearance hadn't slipped, but without another look in the mirror she couldn't be sure. In any case, this was what they called hitting the ground running.

"Now, as far as scheduling for the fall," he went on, "you know we're having a regular staff meeting about that tomorrow morning. I want you to run that meeting."

"Run the meeting. Sure. I'll be happy to do that."

She had never run a meeting before—at least not one like this, with all the staff and everyone watching her to see if she could handle it. What if she fell on her face? And how was she supposed to relate to her fellow teachers now? She added a couple more items to her to-do list. They would need a printed agenda as well as a worksheet on which they could all collaborate to create a working schedule. She almost bumped into a cluster of girls from her former class.

"Hi, Mrs. Stevenson." One of the girls, a junior named Morgan, looked up at her with a big smile.

At first it didn't register what they were saying, and then it suddenly occurred to her that Pete's mom must have stepped into the building without her noticing. Dana almost missed the moment—until the rest of the girls giggled, and then it *really* registered. Oh, right. *She* was Mrs. Stevenson.

"Hi, girls." She paused, giving them a chance to shower her with questions about the honeymoon.

Dana indulged them to a point and then changed the subject. "Your sub told you what's going on, right? That I won't be teaching the class for the rest of the year?"

They nodded in unison while several of the girls put on sour expressions.

"But it's not fair," said Morgan. "We thought you were just going on your honeymoon, and now you're bailing on us for good."

"I'm not bailing on you," Dana replied, holding out her hands. "See? I'm still right here."

But Morgan frowned and parked her hands on her hips after slamming her locker for effect.

"Does this mean we don't have to do the literature report?" she asked.

"Nice try." Dana told them. "But whatever the sub tells you is what I would have told you too. Same assignments, same due dates, same everything."

The girls did a group moan, but that wasn't going to

change their assignments. By now Mr. Duncan had nearly disappeared down the hall, walking quickly through the thinning crowds. Had he even noticed that Dana had stopped to talk to the girls?

"Uh-oh," Dana told them. "Gotta go!"

As she turned to go she noticed Emily, her newly acquired niece, at the far end of the opposite hall. That wasn't so unusual during passing time between classes, and normally they would wave or say hi to each other. But this time Emily didn't see her, and she certainly didn't realize Dana saw her holding hands with Troy Vanderveen, the tall kid with the scruffy blond hair and the hint of a beard on his chin. Hmm.

Not that Troy wasn't a nice kid. Basically he was. But everyone in the school—staff included—knew of Troy's less-than-stellar reputation. Nice family, bad friends. Excellent head on his shoulders, less-than-excellent choices. A train wreck ready to happen. In fact, Dana would put him in the "great-potential, headed-for-real-trouble" category. And those kinds of kids were personally the most disappointing to her, as well as the most troubling. It didn't have to be.

Emily, however, obviously didn't share her concern. Even from down the hall, Dana couldn't miss the deer-in-the-headlights look she gave the taller boy. By the way he smiled and laughed, Dana could tell he was obviously enjoying every moment of the attention.

Mr. Duncan had finally noticed Dana wasn't following; he stood outside the conference room, waiting with arms crossed as she hurried to catch up.

"Sorry about that," she told him, catching her breath. "Some of the girls in one of my classes were wondering about their assignment."

"I'm sure the substitute gave them all the details they'll need." He checked his watch with a frown. "And actually, you're going to see your relationship with the kids shifting somewhat."

"Shifting from what it has been?" She wasn't sure she knew exactly what he meant.

"That's right. Look, if you're serious about applying for the permanent position, it might behoove you to see yourself as more of a disciplinarian, especially compared to what you have been as a teacher. Are you up for that?"

"Well, yes. Of course." Dana wasn't sure if this was encouragement or a light rebuke.

"Good. Because whoever gets this job is going to be in charge of student discipline issues and interfacing with parents whenever there's an infraction or any other problem."

"I understand." She nodded and then made a two-word note in the margin of her notebook: get tough.

Meanwhile, Mr. Duncan continued with his tour de force of her new job description. "Now, let's talk about the changes we're putting into place for next fall's bus schedules, and then I'll show you our custodial schedule. You're going to need to keep it updated because you'll be the primary contact for building maintenance. Not that you'll have to do any of the maintenance yourself, of course. You'll just keep track of it and make sure it gets done."

"I'm right with you."

At least she was trying to be. She checked over her shoulder one more time, just to see. Emily and her new boyfriend had already disappeared around the corner, and it made her wonder. *Should I talk to Charlotte about what's going on? Or maybe even Pete?*

Perhaps neither. As Emily's aunt, Dana thought perhaps she herself now had a bigger role to play in the girl's life than she had originally realized. But then again, she didn't want to appear like a meddler, offering advice where none was requested and thus burning her bridges or straining her relationship with Emily, which had always been pretty good. Until now, at least.

Sometimes it was easy to forget just how much Emily had been through, what with losing her mother and not having her father around. Lots of kids came from broken homes and less-than-ideal situations, but Emily's case hit close to home. It was hard for her even to imagine the pain this poor girl had been through. No wonder she was susceptible to getting into a lopsided relationship with an older kid with a "bad boy" reputation. When Dana thought about it that way, it made much more sense.

Charlotte and Bob were doing a great job, but no one could replace a child's mother.

"Something wrong?" asked Mr. Duncan, still holding the door open for her. Had he been talking about the bus schedule? "You seem a little . . . distracted."

"No, no. Not at all. I'm just, you know, there's a lot to process."

Perhaps she shouldn't have said it that way, especially with all the confidence Mr. Duncan had placed in her. But he smiled for the first time that morning and seemed to lighten up a notch or two.

"I know this is a lot of new territory, Dana, but you're

going to catch right on. Even so, you tell me if I'm going too fast or if you have any questions, okay? Now, about the bus schedule . . ."

She nodded her head yes, forcing herself to return to the moment and clearing her mind of all the unbidden thoughts about Emily. Whew! What was that all about? She hadn't been promoted to school guidance counselor yet, though hadn't Mr. Duncan mentioned something about that too? For now, and with everything he was dumping on her plate, she had more than enough to keep her occupied. So she scribbled a few more notes and followed him into the conference room, where a few of the other staff members were already waiting.

DANA DIDN'T HAVE A CHANCE to catch her breath until several hours later, when she gathered her things into her leather briefcase and finally headed for the parking lot. Eddie the janitor paused at his floor-buffing machine to give her a smile and a wave.

"I hear you're going to be my new boss, Miss Simons." He switched off the buffer and brushed away a wisp of his thin gray hair. Or what was left of it. "I mean, sorry, Mrs. Stevenson. Gotta get used to that new name, right?"

"I'm still getting used to it myself." She smiled back at him. And yes, it was going to take some getting used to thinking of herself as Eddie's supervisor. "But please, my name is still just Dana. That works best for me."

"Sure thing, just Dana." He grinned as he switched on the orbital buffer once more, leaving her to walk down the hallway alone. And though she had often worked long days in the classroom, a wall of exhaustion now turned her legs to lead, and she could hardly hold up her head.

And when she looked at the clock in the reception area, at first she thought surely it had stopped that morning. One more maintenance item to mention to Eddie.

Then it hit her: *It can't be 7 PM!*

Yet it was. And it hit her that Pete would once again be waiting for her at home, probably warming up another pizza. Despite her fatigue she quickened her step, grabbing a pile of papers, memos, and pink "while you were out" message slips from her overflowing mailbox. Her new mailbox, actually. Someone had already added an additional label to her new name: Dana Stevenson, acting assistant principal.

Despite her fatigue and despite one of the most intense days she'd experienced since final exams back in college, she smiled as she stood alone in the silent, empty front office.

Acting assistant principal sounded pretty good.

One of the phone message slips fluttered to the floor, and she reached to pick it up. She caught her breath when she saw the note.

Your husband called, wants you to call back when you're free.

Oh! The note was from that morning.

Another slip carried the same message, but it had been left at noon, when she'd had a busy lunch meeting with the district superintendent.

Yet another message from Pete at 3:10, just after classes

were normally dismissed; she often called him then to see what was happening that evening. Today she'd been immersed in a planning session, however. Her heart sank as she held the handful of slips and checked the wall clock once more, just to be sure. But it wasn't broken.

She quickly turned and hurried for the front door. Pete would understand how busy she'd become.

Wouldn't he?

Chapter Eleven

P lease please *please*, Grandma?" Emily folded her hands and gave Charlotte what looked to be her best puppy-dog expression—with sad eyes and long face. "You know how many hours of practice I need before I can get my license."

"Yes, you need that, as well as your sixteenth birthday."

"But I'm turning sixteen in just five days. This Sunday."

"Really? I'd forgotten all about that."

Charlotte could tease a little too sometimes.

"Grandma, come on. You don't forget anything."

Charlotte didn't mind that Emily was eager to drive. She looked up from stirring her batch of brownies. "Well, as I recall, it has always been your grandfather's job to do the driver's training."

"But Grandpa's always out on his tractor this time of year. He's busy with the planting."

"You're right about that. But you should have seen the way he trained your uncles, first out in the field on the tractor and then around the farm in the truck before he finally felt they were ready for an actual road. He was a good teacher."

"Maybe back then. Now he always acts like he's either too busy or too tired."

"Don't be too hard on him. He works harder than he should."

"So why doesn't he ease up?"

"You should ask him that yourself."

"If he ever comes in."

"Hmm. I'm afraid you may have a point. How about your Uncle Pete? I'll bet he'd be happy to ride along with you. He probably remembers what it was like to get his driver's license, since it was a lot more recent."

"You think fifteen years ago is recent?"

"You'd be surprised. To you it's a lifetime. At my age, it's nothing."

"But he's too busy working on his house."

"Which is why your grandfather has been working so hard in the fields lately."

Charlotte frowned as she added a little more oil to her brownie mix for good measure, and then resumed her stirring.

"Grandma?"

"All right, all right. I need to get a few things at Herko's anyway. Just give me a chance to finish this up, and then I'll take you out."

Emily brightened.

Twenty minutes later Charlotte sat stiffly in the passenger seat of her little Ford while Emily smiled and turned the key.

"Remember," Charlotte told her, "you want to adjust the mirrors and the seat *before* you place it in gear, not after.

Make sure there's no one around the car who could get hurt."

"You mean like little brothers?" Emily put the car into reverse.

"Especially little brothers. And—"

Gravel flew when Emily suddenly stepped on the brakes. Charlotte's neck whipped around. What in the world?

"Hey, watch out!" Emily hollered as she rolled down the window.

Christopher—the little brother in question—almost looked as if he'd been *trying* to get in the way. From outside and a little behind the car, he waved his arms wildly and play-acted as if he'd been hit.

"Emily's driving!" he squealed. "We're all going to die."

"Christopher!" Now it was Charlotte's turn to settle things down as she leaned out her own window. "We're just going to Herko's for some groceries. You can let Uncle Pete know if there's anything you need."

"Like what? He's working on his house."

"All right. Then I'm sure Grandpa can help you. Only don't wander off. Why don't you go check on Magic—he's getting better, isn't he? And don't hurt yourself while we're gone."

"I'm not the one who's going to get hurt, Grandma. You're riding with her."

"Hey!" Emily objected. "Wait 'til you start driving. I'll bet you get in a wreck before you—"

"All right, you two," said Charlotte. "Nobody's getting hurt. And if Grandpa or Uncle Pete want to know, you tell them we just went to the store and we'll be right back."

Emily stepped on the accelerator—and backed into one of the large rose bushes bordering the back step, making an alarming sound like fingernails dragging across a chalkboard. Charlotte cringed but tried not to overreact.

"Sorry, Grandma." Emily turned a little red in the face, put the car in drive, and moved forward. Well, everyone had to learn at some point. Maybe it was a good thing Bob wasn't here to see this. Christopher laughed and pointed, but by that time they had both rolled up their windows and were ignoring him.

"All right." Charlotte pointed toward the main road. "Let's just move down the driveway and turn toward Bedford. Carefully. Focus."

"I'm a camera," said Emily between a nervous smile and pursed lips.

"Not too fast." Charlotte didn't want to imagine everything that could go wrong when an inexperienced one-hundred-pound teenager piloted a twenty-five-hundred-pound vehicle down the highway—and none too expertly, at that. Without thinking about it, she found herself stomping on the floorboard as they came to the end of the driveway.

"Don't panic, Grandma."

Emily must have thought it was funny. But really, Charlotte found nothing amusing about this scenario. This was all about survival. She wondered how much of a difference airbags would make—and then remembered her car didn't have them. At least Emily put on the right-turn blinker without being reminded, even though they were still a long way from the highway.

"You're doing fine so far." Now Charlotte used her most

soothing voice as a way of preventing the obvious tension in the car from taking over. When they got to the highway, she said, "Check both ways and then, when it's clear, ease into traffic."

That sounded like the appropriate thing to say in a situation such as this. However, the only thing that could be considered "traffic" was Walt Freeman's tractor just ahead, tooling along at about 10 miles per hour. Emily drove up behind him, looked nervously into the oncoming lane, and didn't seem to know what to do.

"There's no one coming, Emily," Charlotte told her. "You can pull around when you see it's clear."

That was easier said than done. But after some effort they finally continued on their way to town. Charlotte did her best not to grip the dashboard with white knuckles and tried not to make too many critical comments about Emily's speed, about checking the mirror, or about watching for crossing traffic.

Maybe a little casual conversation will help ease the tension, she thought as they approached town. But what to say?

"How's school lately?" she asked.

"Fine. School is fine."

Emily's eyes were glued to the road ahead, and she kept a death grip on the steering wheel. Charlotte would have to try something else.

"How about your friends?"

"Fine. Friends are fine."

So maybe Emily wasn't in the mood to talk while she was driving. Or maybe it was a good time for a woman-to-woman talk. She thought, *What could it hurt? When do I have a chance like this, with a captive audience?*

She decided to ask.

"I hear you've been getting to know Troy Vanderveen."

At first Emily didn't answer, but even from the passenger seat Charlotte could sense her granddaughter's neck muscles tightening. She had obviously hit a nerve.

"He's just a friend," Emily finally whispered.

"Oh." But Charlotte decided she might not get another chance. "A good friend?"

Emily sighed before responding again. "Why is everybody so against him?"

"Who said anyone was against him?" Charlotte tried to sound as neutral as possible. "I just asked—"

"Everybody is always saying he's trouble, and I don't think he is. He's really sweet when he's around me. We talk about lots of things. He asks me questions. He listens to what I say too. He's really funny."

"You've been spending time with him?"

This time Emily looked over at her, pulling the wheel over as she did. With squealing tires they nearly drove off the side of Heather Creek Road. A car behind them flashed by, horn blaring.

"Emily!" Charlotte shouted, grabbing the wheel to straighten them out. "Keep your eyes on the road!"

"I am! But you're distracting me!"

"I am not doing anything of the sort. I just—"

By this time Emily was so flustered she actually had to pull over, and Charlotte reached over to switch off the ignition before anything worse could happen. Goodness! This certainly was not the way she had intended to give her granddaughter driving lessons. But she had nearly driven poor Emily to tears.

"Don't cry, dear." For a moment Charlotte thought she might break down as well. "I shouldn't have brought up the subject. I honestly just wanted to know about the boy, and I don't want you to be hurt."

"That's what I was trying to tell you. He's not like that. He's not going to hurt me or anybody else, no matter what people say about him. But I don't want to talk about it anymore right now."

"I didn't mean to say anything negative about Troy. But please remember that we're not sitting at the kitchen table back home. You're behind the wheel of a car, and you need to pay attention, no matter what."

"Then let's not talk about it, OK?" Emily bit her lip and stared at the road as several trucks and a couple of minutes passed by.

"All right. I was just trying to make you feel more comfortable. Perhaps that was the wrong approach. I'm sorry."

Emily seemed to think about that for a few more moments.

"I didn't mean to flip out, Grandma," she finally said in a very small voice. "Maybe can we just have a do-over?"

"That's a very good idea. You drive carefully, and we can talk about Troy Vanderveen some other time. Truce?"

"Fine with me. Truce." Emily nodded and kept a straight face as she wiped a tear with her sleeve, much the way Bill or Pete might have done when they were younger and didn't want anyone to think something had hurt them, when it really had.

"All right then." Charlotte tried to read Emily's expression but couldn't. "Let's pretend none of this happened.

Let's have you start up the car again and then check your mirrors for traffic while you put on your left turn signal."

"Start car, check." Emily took a deep breath and restarted the car. "Check mirrors, check. Turn on right blinker, check."

"You mean left."

"Left, right."

Despite the touch of silliness, this time Emily sounded all business. Charlotte guessed it might be awhile before her granddaughter would soften enough to talk again about Troy Vanderveen. Or any other boy, for that matter.

Lord, I certainly made a mess of things, didn't I? she prayed.

She thought this would be a perfect time for a do-over of her own.

Chapter
Twelve

Wednesday afternoon Christopher threaded his way through all the kids scrambling to get a ride home after school, like he was, or hurrying to find their bus. A few who lived in town headed for their bikes or simply walked down Lincoln Street.

Once in a while Christopher thought it might be cool to live in town, close to school and to baseball games or Kepler's Pharmacy, where they could get candy anytime they wanted. On the other hand, if they lived in town they probably wouldn't have a fun barn to explore, and they couldn't raise cool animals like Magic—even though Christopher was pretty sure something was still wrong with him.

Besides, if he had to get to school on his bike, like Dylan did, he wouldn't get to ride in his brother's cool little Datsun 240-Z sports car. Even though it was way old and rusty and loud and had had about ten different paint jobs, everyone thought it was cool. It was so cool, in fact, that Christopher didn't mind that he usually had to ride in the little backseat, which really wasn't a backseat at all but more of a storage area behind the two front seats.

Sam pulled up in the parking area right on time, and Christopher climbed aboard.

"You mean I get to sit in the front seat this time?" asked Christopher. "What happened to Emily?"

"She's getting a ride with Ashley." Sam grabbed a couple of schoolbooks and tossed them to the backseat. "Guess they're working on something."

"Cool." That was fine with Christopher. "Do you think—"

"Hold on a sec." Sam held up a hand when his cell phone rang; he kept talking to someone as they slowly pulled away. Christopher thought to remind his brother that he really wasn't supposed to talk on the phone while he drove and that it was against the law in California, Connecticut, D.C., New York, Washington State, and probably a bunch more places by now, but he couldn't remember which ones.

Instead he strapped himself in and enjoyed the view from the front seat until Sam hung up.

Hey, without Emily in the car, maybe they could have a real man-to-man talk. Maybe they could figure out a way to have Sam stay home in the fall instead of going off to college, the way Grandma had been saying. Christopher tried to think of a way to bring it up.   °

"I'll bet you could make lots of money if you got a full-time job around here, couldn't you?" he said.

Sam frowned and glanced over at him.

"What kind of job you talking about?"

"Uh . . ." Christopher's mind went blank. "I don't know. Like what you've been doing, only you'd work more and they would pay you more? Then you could, you know, stay around."

Sam shook his head and smiled.

"Wish it was that easy," he said, but then he changed the subject too quickly. "Hey, what's up with that lamb of yours? Is he eating anything yet?"

"Sort of, but still not as much as my 4-H leader says he should. You think maybe I should feed him something different?"

Sam was about to answer when his cell phone rang again, which only made Christopher think of how to invent a portable cell-phone jamming device. He could keep it in his backpack, and when people around him were talking too long (like Sam did, or Emily), he would just press a button, and his little jammer would stop them from being able to talk. Yeah, he wished he could invent something like that. Maybe if he read a couple more books about inventing or about electronics, he could invent it.

They cruised down Lincoln Street, Sam still gabbing in the sort of goofy tone of voice that made Christopher think it was probably Arielle and not somebody like Grandma.

"Nah, it's just me and my little brother," said Sam. "She had to stay after school to do some kind of math assignment with Ashley. At least that's what she told me. So she's going to get a ride with—"

He paused when the person on the other end of the line interrupted him and then shifted the cell phone to his other ear.

"What are you talking about? You just saw Ashley at the restaurant? You mean Emily's not—"

Sam's eyes kind of bugged out at that point, like the

other person was telling him some big news or something he didn't know.

"All right, thanks. Yeah, I'll check there. I'm going to find out what's going on. Later."

He snapped his cell phone shut and tossed it onto Christopher's lap. Then, with a quick glance in the cracked rearview mirror, he hung a quick U-turn in the middle of Lincoln Street, sending Christopher almost through his door. Good thing he had his seat belt on.

"What's going on?" asked Christopher.

"That's what I'm going to find out." Sam had his jaw set and his eyebrows scrunched. He wasn't messing around. "Arielle says Ashley isn't doing math with Emily the way she said they were going to do."

"Huh?" Christopher ran through the options. Either his sister was lying to them, or she was very mixed up. "Why would Emily say they were doing math if they're not?"

Sam just shook his head as they headed right back the way they had come. Soon they pulled up in front of the high school—directly across the street from Christopher's school.

By this time all the buses were pretty much gone, and so were most of the kids. The only ones left were the ones playing baseball in the field next to the school and a few other kids who were trying out for a Science Olympiad thing Christopher had heard of but wouldn't be old enough for until maybe next year. He thought it sounded cool though, especially if he could do something on weather science.

Sam stopped the car with a little bit of a tire squeal and hopped out.

"Stay here," he told Christopher, not waiting for an answer. But no way was Christopher going to miss out. He followed his big brother inside and didn't say anything.

Good thing too because Christopher was the first to see their sister at the far end of the hall, past a bank of lockers. Christopher noticed she was holding a big kid's hand, but she let go just as they came around the corner. Sam was looking the other way, so Christopher elbowed his brother and pointed.

"There she is," he told Sam. They waited right there for her, hands on their hips, as the other guy waved at Emily and kind of peeled off in the other direction. She looked a little surprised when she approached them.

"What are you guys doing here?" she asked. She stood lop-sided because of all the weight in her backpack, but at the same time she was all smiley and bubbly, which didn't make much sense to Christopher. Grandma said she thought Emily's back was going to go crooked on account of all those books.

"What are *we* doing here?" asked Sam. "What are *you* doing here?" He didn't take his hands from his hips or change the serious look on his face. All he needed was a dark uniform and a gun in his holster.

"But I told you I was going to get a ride." She still looked confused about the boys being at the school, like they should not have come back to rescue her. "I hope you didn't wait here."

"We didn't wait," said Sam.

"We came back," added Christopher. Now he was getting kind of interested in hearing what she was going to say, or how she was going to explain this. But by the look on her face, she still didn't seem to understand.

"How was your math assignment?" asked Sam, like he was trying to be a CSI detective.

"Oh, that!" Now she seemed to get it. "Ashley is such a flake sometimes. I even reminded her probably ten times today. I was like, 'After school at the library, right?' And she was like, 'No problem.' But then she never showed. What else could I do?"

She didn't look disappointed at all. Sam looked like he was about to tell her what else she could do, but instead he just shook his head as they walked back down the hall and out the door. She paused in front of the car.

"It's too bad I can't drive," she said, looking hopefully at the driver's side of the little car. Was she changing the subject? "You don't think you could—"

"Don't even think about it. After all the grief I got the other day just for riding with Paul, no way am I going to let you drive my car with just your learner's permit."

"But it's only three more days," she said, but without much conviction. Instead she slipped into the backseat and let Christopher sit in front—without even arguing, for the first time in history.

Whoa, thought Christopher, *maybe she's sick or something*.

If she was, she was goofy-sick. And as they pulled away from the school she looked back out the window. Christopher noticed that guy again, sort of waving at her, underhanded. Like nobody was going to notice?

This time Sam must have seen it in his rearview mirror

too. And even though he hadn't seen her holding hands in the hallway, he could probably tell what was going on.

"I saw you riding around in Troy Vanderveen's car the other night," Sam blurted out. "I mean, you think people don't know, like it's some kind of secret. But we're not stupid, Emily."

"Well, neither am I."

"He's a jerk, Emily. A total jerk. He and those guys he hangs around with trashed a bunch of benches at the city park last fall. Spray-painted them and everything. You really shouldn't—"

"How do you know it was him?" she countered, and Christopher could only watch as the argument heated up. "He says he didn't have anything to do with that."

"Oh, so you asked him? Emily, of all the guys in the school, you have to go and pick a guy who's a year older than you and who's had a bunch of girlfriends. You go and pick the juvenile delinquent."

"You're starting to sound just like Grandpa."

"Well, it's true. Everybody knows."

"Everybody knows nothing. Troy is really nice to me."

"Huh. Just like those mafia guys on TV. They do a hit on somebody, blood all over the place, and then they go home and they're all nice to their little kids, like nothing happened. It's just like that."

"This is nuts. Troy is not the mafia."

"Believe me, Emily. Around here, he is."

"You can't be serious."

"You're the one who can't be serious, Emily."

And on it went, back and forth. Up ahead, a big tanker

truck had slowed down on the road. Christopher dug his fingernails into the dashboard. "Uh, Sam," he said, raising his own voice to be heard above the argument. He tapped his brother on the shoulder. "You might want to take a look at the road ahead of us."

"What?" Sam looked just in time, slamming on the brakes to keep from rear-ending the truck. That would not have been good. Emily grunted when she bumped her face against the back of Sam's seat.

"All right, that's it. I don't need this." She shoved the seat and her big brother forward into the steering wheel, managing to grab the door handle and yank it upward, and then slip through the narrow space and escape to the street outside.

Sam, red-faced, pulled over and put the car in park, flipped on the hazard flashers, and got out to follow her.

"Get back in the car, Emily," he said.

"You're a menace," she answered, still striding down the sidewalk, heading back toward school. "I hope for Christopher's sake you don't have an accident."

"You're worse," he countered. "And you'd better not get a ride home with that guy."

"Why not?" she tossed her head and pointed her nose at the sky. "He's a much better driver than you are."

That was apparently all Sam could take.

"Fine," he said, stopping where he was. "I'll just tell Grandma who you're with, and who you were with the other night, instead of being at Ashley's. I didn't say anything before, you know."

That got her, and she stopped right there on the sidewalk with a frozen look on her face. After a moment Emily stepped back to Sam's car and climbed back in from Christopher's side.

"It's not like you think," she explained as she returned to her little seat and folded her arms across her chest. "He was just giving me a ride to Ashley's that night. That's all."

Sam didn't say anything, just fumed instead. Christopher could almost see the smoke coming out of his ears; he didn't dare make a peep. They left town and continued down Heather Creek Road. Christopher was tired of talking about Troy Vanderveen. He wanted to talk about someone else. "Hey, when we get home, do you want to go with me to see if Magic is doing better?" he asked, changing the subject.

Sam just stared at the road ahead while Emily glared out the little side window. Neither answered him, and neither said anything the rest of the ride home. Maybe they hadn't heard.

Chapter
Thirteen

Come on, fella. What's wrong with you?"
Christopher held a bowl of feed in front of Magic's cute black face, but the silly lamb only turned away and made his sheep sounds, like he was hurting, and then he wobbled like he wasn't sure about standing up. Why didn't he ever act hungry?

Christopher thought maybe they should keep him in the pen inside the barn all the time instead of letting him roam around the big fenced area right next to the barn. Maybe it would help to keep him inside. Maybe he was just scared of being outside.

Sheep weren't supposed to be scared outside so it had to be something else, Christopher thought. Problem was, Christopher had no idea what it could be. He dropped to his knees just outside the fence and poked a finger through the boards, trying to get Magic's attention. But the lamb just stared straight ahead and tottered. It was getting worse. It just wasn't right.

He heard someone coming up the driveway, but it sounded different than any of their trucks. Grandma had just left to go visit her friend Mrs. Carter. Sam wouldn't be back already since he had gone off to hang out with his friends again. Uncle Pete and Grandpa were off some-place in Sawchuck's Quarter. Only he and Emily were home. Curious, he got up to peek around the corner of the building.

A shiny black pickup had pulled into the driveway, and Christopher trotted toward the house to check things out. The owner of the truck spotted him right away and flashed a big smile.

"Hey," said the visitor, who turned out to be the older kid who had been holding Emily's hand at school. He was pretty tall and had lots of muscles on his arms. And like a lot of high school kids around Bedford, he wore pointy-toed cowboy boots and a baseball cap plus a T-shirt with a rock band logo. Christopher could never figure out those boots, especially why anybody would want to wear them.

"You must be Christopher," said the older boy.

That kind of surprised Christopher, and he stopped for a minute to figure things out.

"How did you know?" Christopher checked out the shiny truck and ran his finger along some of the chrome trim. This guy sure must have spent a lot of time polishing it. And his teeth were almost as shiny as his chrome, kind of like a salesman at a computer store.

"Oh, your sister tells me all about you. Good things, by the way. Your animals, your weather station. She home?"

Christopher didn't have to answer. Emily popped out of the back door just then; she looked pretty glad to see the guy.

"Troy!" She smiled her greeting. "I didn't think I'd see you again so soon."

Yeah, this must be the Troy Vanderveen everybody had

been talking about so much lately, Christopher thought. The one Sam was all worried about. And if Sam was worried about him, maybe Christopher ought to be worried about him too. He eyed the newcomer carefully. The guy smelled kind of funny, like smoke.

"Actually, I found this in my truck," said Troy, reaching into the cab and pulling out a sweater. "Yours, right? I had to take some stuff to my Uncle Walt next door and thought as long as I was out this way, I might as well drop it off."

Emily seemed happy to get her sweater back, but Christopher wasn't so sure.

"My grandma's going to be home any minute," he blurted out. He figured that was probably what Sam would have said. Emily's frown confirmed it for him. "And Emily's probably too busy with homework."

"I am not too busy, thank you," countered Emily. "But Christopher, don't you need to go take care of your lamb?"

Christopher was about to tell her no, that he'd done as much as he could do for the afternoon. But Troy turned to him with a look of excitement.

"No way!" he said. "You raise sheep? Four-H? I used to have a lamb when I was your age. I called him Bucky. I still remember that stubborn old—"

"Magic isn't stubborn," explained Christopher, in case anybody wanted to know. "I think he's just getting sick and won't eat anything."

"Really? Show me where he is, and let's take a look. Oh, and I'm Troy, by the way."

"Christopher." He felt a little silly telling the boy his name after the guy had already said he knew who he was. But anyway, this was the first time anybody had ever asked to actually see Magic, and Christopher really didn't mind showing him. So he led the way to the pen behind the barn as Emily and Troy followed and chatted.

"Yeah," explained Troy, "I had a couple of sheep and some goats too. Kept me busy when I was a kid. How long have you had this one?"

Christopher explained where they got Magic and then answered a couple more questions about his feed and water, that kind of thing. Troy nodded and actually seemed to listen—which was more than Sam and Emily did half the time. What was Sam so worried about again? When they got to the pen, Troy got as close as he could and crouched down for a better view.

"Mine had pneumonia," he told Christopher. "They say a lot of lambs get it. Has he been out in the rain? You might need to get some antibiotics into him."

"Antibiotics, yeah." That sounded good to Christopher. If it helped Magic not be so sick, he was all for it.

But Troy looked a little more concerned when he walked around the fenced area toward a low, marshy spot. He bent down and picked at a couple of weeds growing next to a fence post.

"You let your lamb out here?" he asked, taking a stick and digging at a small plant that looked like a fern. Well, Christopher thought the answer was pretty obvious. He also wasn't totally sure he liked the way Troy asked the question.

"Sometimes we do. He likes to run."

"Yeah, well, if he keeps eating this stuff, he's not going to be running much anymore. You got a pair of gloves?"

"What is it?" Now Emily sounded curious, but Christopher

ran to the barn and returned with a pair of Grandpa's work gloves. Troy slipped them on and quickly yanked a couple of the tiny ferns by the fencepost, and then held them up for Christopher to see.

"This is Nebraska fern," he told him. "I had some of this in the back of our field. Some people call it poison hemlock. It likes wet or marshy places. But it killed one of my goats before I found it."

"You mean—" Christopher looked more closely at the weed. It sure looked like something Magic might have been munching on.

"Poisonous, dude. I know this one's really small, and you probably didn't even know it was here. But even a few bites of this can take out your sheep, or make him really sick. And you don't want to be touching it either. It's nasty stuff."

"Whoa." Christopher was impressed. "You think that's what's bothering him?"

"I wouldn't be surprised. Maybe he nibbled some by accident. But then again, some sheep are pretty weird like that sometimes, eating stuff that's really bad for them. You never can tell. But go ahead and feed him some extra molasses. That should help if he needs more vitamins. And if you see any more weeds like this, be sure to pull them up. See the shape of these leaves?"

He pointed out the leaf with the toe of his boot and handed over the gloves, which Christopher gingerly accepted.

"OK. I know what to do. Thanks."

Now Christopher was totally confused, but not about

the weeds. He slipped on the gloves as he scouted the fence line for any more of the yucky stuff. What exactly didn't Sam like about this guy Troy? As far as Christopher was concerned, he was pretty nice.

"THAT WAS REALLY NICE OF YOU." Emily kept up with Troy as they returned to his truck. "I think you made a new friend."

"You mean that lamb? Yeah, me and sheep." He held up his hand with two fingers crossed. "We're like this."

"No, silly." She laughed and leaned against him as they walked. "I mean Christopher. That was nice of you to help him out. He's been worried about that lamb ever since he got him. We thought he was just freaking over nothing. But he didn't know about any poisonous weeds. None of us did."

"No problem." Troy shrugged as they stepped up to his truck. "Here, you want to practice a little driving?"

She looked uncertainly at him and then at his nice truck. "Are you sure?"

"Sure I'm sure. You need to take your driving test in a few days, don't you?"

"Well, if my grandparents let me."

"And do you know how to parallel park? I'll bet you don't. They're going to make you do it during the driving test, and you don't want to go crashing into any cars in town."

"Actually, Grandma and I haven't done parallel parking yet. She says she's not sure how to teach it to me."

He grabbed a couple of flowerpots from the back porch and set them about fifteen feet apart on the gravel driveway next to the house.

"Let's see if you can park in between these two pots," he told her, tossing her the keys. "This will be like a car in front and a car behind, and you've just found a parking space. What are you going to do?"

A moment later she sat in the driver's seat next to him. The dashboard gleamed as if it had been sprayed with that leather cleaner stuff, but she could also detect a faint whiff of smoke. Troy pushed the ashtray closed.

"That's from my cousin," he said, looking a little sheepish. "He borrowed the truck the other day and left his cigarette butts, if you can believe it."

He snapped on the radio, tuned to a country station. "Oh." Still she wrinkled her nose—not so much at the music, but at the stale smoke smell. But she liked that it wasn't his fault after all. And even if it had been, she reasoned, maybe that would not have been such a major big deal. Would it? She just wouldn't tell Grandma, who would have a definite opinion about it.

Compared to Grandma's little car, the pickup's steering wheel felt enormous and a little, well, overwhelming. Everything in the truck felt a little overwhelming.

"Hey, it's not a rodeo," he told her. "You don't need to wrestle it to the ground. Just turn it smoothly."

She giggled nervously as she pulled up past the flowerpot and stopped, and then switched into reverse and cranked the wheel.

"A little more," he said, coaching her. She went through

the motions several more times and only knocked over the pots a couple of times. Troy never seemed to get excited when she did. But she still hadn't actually managed to park the truck correctly.

"How am I doing?" she asked the sixth time she maneuvered back and forth, trying to get into the parking spot. Or the seventh; she was losing track.

"You'll get it this next time," he told her, still smiling. "Here, why don't you straighten out and try again?"

She could do that. Not only did she straighten out, but she also drove on down the driveway for good measure. A quick look in the rearview told her Grandpa and Uncle Pete were nowhere near, although she thought she saw Christopher still running around by the barn. Oh well. He would be fine by himself for a little while. A minute later they approached Heather Creek Road and she voiced her crazy idea.

"I could always use more driving practice out there," she said, looking at him out of the corner of her eye.

She bit her tongue when he didn't answer right away and gripped the steering wheel even more tightly. She closed her eyes as they sat idling at the end of the drive.

I should never have said that! She scolded herself and wished she could take back what she'd said. Finally he broke the silence by turning up the radio.

"Uh, I'd like to," he said, sounding a little iffy. "But your grandma would kill me if she knew I took you out on the highway. Besides, I think officially I have to be eighteen to drive with you when you only have a learner's permit, and I'm not quite there yet."

"Right, dumb idea." Emily was quick to chime back. "I should never have suggested it."

"No, no. Like I said, I'd really like to take you out driving. You're a good driver. I mean, once we get this parallel parking thing down, you'll be great. Maybe in a few weeks, when you get your license?"

A few *weeks*? She felt a little red in the face but nodded her agreement as she turned the truck around and headed back toward the house. Christopher had disappeared, and she wished she could do the same.

Chapter
Fourteen

Charlotte hadn't meant to eavesdrop, but when she went upstairs that evening for a couple of clean sheets out of the linen closet, she really couldn't avoid overhearing. And the two of them, Emily and Christopher, really weren't keeping their voices down, were they?

"I'm going to tell," said Christopher.

"No, you're not." Emily's voice heated up. She obviously wasn't about to let him get away with anything. "And besides, there's nothing to tell."

"But I saw you driving out to the road. You're not supposed to drive out on the road without an adult."

"Did you see me drive out *on* the road?" Now Emily put on her trial lawyer voice.

"Well . . . you were going in that direction. And you were in his truck."

"There's nothing wrong with being in his truck. And you didn't actually see us turn onto Heather Creek Road, did you?"

"You were gone a long time."

"You didn't answer my question. You were taking care of your lamb on the other side of the barn. You couldn't see very well from over there. So did you actually see us turn onto Heather Creek Road?"

Charlotte couldn't help leaning a little closer to hear the verdict.

"Not really," replied Christopher, and his voice had retreated by now. "But—"

"But nothing. You didn't see us turn onto the road because we stayed on the driveway. And there's nothing illegal about staying on the driveway, is there?"

"Why would you drive all the way down the driveway if you weren't going to go out on the road?"

"Don't answer a question with a question."

"Aw, come on, Emily. I'm tired of this. I'm still going to tell Grandma unless you help with my chores."

"Now you're blackmailing me. Where did you learn how to do that?"

"It was on an episode of *True Crime Stories* on TV. There was this famous singer guy, and one of his fans wanted to get a lot of money out of him, so—"

"All right, all right. I really didn't want the whole story. And I'll do your chores for you tonight, but that's all."

"Today and tomorrow, or no deal."

"You awful little worm. Get out of my room."

"Or I'll tell Grandma and Grandpa that you're going out with your boyfriend on your birthday instead of having a party with us."

"What? How did you know that?"

"You're always talking on your phone. I hear things."

"Out! You little spy. Get out of here!"

Charlotte didn't move quickly enough to get away from the door; she was still trying to get over what she'd heard.

Emily's *boyfriend*? What had been happening here this afternoon while Charlotte was visiting with Hannah? Unfortunately, she had nowhere to turn when Christopher burst into the hall and ran straight into her. He let out a yelp of surprise as they collided, landing on the floor and nearly bowling Charlotte over too.

"Uh-oh." Christopher looked up at Charlotte, who had almost dropped the linens. Then he looked back over his shoulder at Emily. "I won't tell, Emily."

Emily stood framed in the doorway, her arms crossed.

"Doesn't matter, Christopher," she said in a monotone, with a frown to match. "I'm sure she heard everything."

Now Christopher scrambled to his feet.

"Did you, Grandma? Even the part about Emily driving Troy Vanderveen's black truck?"

"I-I just came up to get some linens," she answered, stumbling a bit over her words. "But yes, you two were discussing things rather loudly."

Emily tried to slam her door, but it caught on Christopher's foot and he yelped loudly enough to get Bob's attention downstairs.

"What's going on up there?" he hollered up the stairwell. "Sounds like someone's butchering a pig."

Well, not quite. But if Emily's looks could kill . . .

"I didn't do anything wrong, Grandma," she finally said, still gripping the doorknob of her bedroom door, which was locked in a stalemate with Christopher's leg.

"You didn't tell us you had a boy over." Charlotte decided the best course would be to get it out in the open right here and right now. No use putting it off anymore.

"I didn't invite him. He just came." Once more Emily

tried to shut her door, but Christopher had stationed him-self on the doorjamb so she couldn't.

"And who are we talking about here?" Charlotte just now began to put the pieces together. "You're not really seeing the Vanderveen boy, are you?"

"What if I am?" Emily hadn't lost her argumentative tone from when she had been scolding her little brother. "What would be so wrong with that?"

"Dear, isn't he a senior?" Charlotte wasn't sure she wanted to get into this discussion, but it seemed inevitable. She could see in Emily's eyes the same flinty resistance Denise had once shown. Like mother, like daughter. "He must be two years older than you."

"Actually he's only a junior, and he's still seventeen." Now Emily took up her arguing pose, hand on her hip and chin stuck out defiantly. Again, just like her mother used to do, once upon a time. Charlotte wished Bob would come back her up, but then she thought maybe Emily would react even more defensively if it were two against one. So she just tried to remain calm, although it felt like a losing battle.

"Still, older boys sometimes take advantage of situations like that, you know."

Immediately Charlotte regretted saying such a thing in front of Christopher. Her eyes met his, and she was relieved to see that he didn't understand her meaning. But Emily did, and it only seemed to make her angrier than she already was.

"You're not being fair! He's not like that! He's the one who made me do the right thing."

Now it was Emily's turn to rue her words. She caught her breath with a little gasp and brought a hand to her lips. She had obviously not meant to say that. Charlotte set her linens back on the shelf of the linen closet and turned back toward the kids to face the situation squarely, with or without Bob's help. Meanwhile, Emily still had words for her little brother.

"Don't you say a word," she warned him, wagging a finger in his direction. "This is none of your business."

"All right, all right," he answered, crossing his arms in defeat.

Charlotte wasn't sure how to handle this fight, but she did know it wouldn't help to drag Christopher into the middle of things.

"Christopher," she asked, "don't you have some chores to do?"

"But—" He looked up at his sister with wide eyes.

"She's not doing anything for you, Christopher." Charlotte looked him right in the eyes and pointed to the stairway. "Now you'd better go and let us figure this out."

He gathered himself up with a sigh and shuffled away, but that only left Charlotte to face her granddaughter alone. And Emily's face had not softened at all, as far as Charlotte could tell. Perhaps another approach would be a good idea.

"All right, let's back up here for a moment. Troy Vanderveen came here to the farm uninvited, this afternoon, is that right?"

Emily frowned but nodded as Charlotte continued.

"And he let you drive his truck?"

"They went down the driveway," said Christopher from halfway down the stairs.

"I told you to go, Christopher, and I expect you to mind!" Charlotte felt her temperature rising all too quickly and heard him stomp down the rest of the stairs. She turned to Emily with the same hands-on-hips pose as her granddaughter.

"Well?" Perhaps she'd raised her voice a bit too much now, but she felt her anger getting away from her and she knew her cheeks were flaming. "He let you drive his truck. Is that right? You know you're only supposed to drive with your grandfather, Uncle Pete, or myself. What do you—"

"It wasn't his fault." Emily interrupted, raising her voice over Charlotte's. By this time tears streamed down her red cheeks. "He was just trying to be nice and I talked him into letting me drive. He helped me parallel park, which you never did, by the way, and then I got the idea to just go driving a little, but he said you'd kill him if he let me, so we didn't, no matter what Christopher tells you. He was all the way across the yard, behind the barn with his lamb, but it doesn't matter, 'cause you're blaming Troy anyway, just like everybody else always does, and it's not fair that everybody always blames him for stuff he doesn't do, because nobody understands, and you don't understand, and Grandpa doesn't understand, and Uncle Pete doesn't understand, and I just hate it!"

With that she turned and threw herself on her bed, ending the confrontation and leaving Charlotte wide-eyed, breathless, and speechless.

What have I done? Charlotte asked herself, and now she wasn't sure if her flaming cheeks were due to her anger or her embarrassment that she had allowed herself to lose her temper.

"I'm sorry, Lord," she whispered, holding her head in

her hands. But she recognized again the awful feeling of what it was like to lose her daughter.

Or rather, her granddaughter. But it seemed to be happening exactly the same way.

"LET ME GIVE YOU some advice, Magic." Christopher sat on a bale of hay inside his lamb's pen, kicking at the loose straw scattered on the floor. The little black lamb paused from chewing his feed and gazed up at him with a look of curious interest. "Stay away from girls. All girls. Sister girls. Girls at school. Teacher girls. Grandma girls. They're all the same. They're all nuts, and nobody can figure them out. So don't even try."

He stood up and gave the straw one last kick, not quite sure what made him so upset, or even why he wanted to punch something. So it was probably a good thing it was just him and Magic, because Magic was a good listener and Emily sure wasn't nice to him. She was just totally sneaky about the whole boyfriend thing and about Troy Vanderveen too, in his humble opinion.

"And you know what else?" he asked the lamb. "If this is the kind of trouble it causes, I'm never going to have a girlfriend. Unless of course she has a cool black truck like Troy Vanderveen, and she lets me drive it. Then I would think about it."

Despite the ache he felt in the pit of his stomach after being yelled at by both Emily and Grandma, he kind of smiled at his little joke, and at the thought of being able to drive a truck like Troy Vanderveen's. Speaking of which, he thought he heard a low rumble from somewhere outside, the same sound he'd heard this afternoon when Troy came.

"Do you hear that, Magic?"

Magic cocked his head to the side but kept chewing.

Yeah, maybe Magic heard it too. Christopher climbed back out of the pen and hurried to the door, just to see what might be going on. Wouldn't that be something if Troy Vanderveen came driving up their driveway again? But this time Grandma would probably come running out and chase him off with a broom.

Well, she probably wouldn't do that, exactly.

When Christopher got outside in the dark he didn't see anyone driving up the driveway. The rumble was from much farther way, in the direction of Uncle Pete's construction site. He could tell, not just from the rumble but also from a set of headlights that flashed in the distance.

That's his truck! thought Christopher. It sure sounded like it anyway. A black truck at this time of night was hard to see. So he waited for a few minutes, straining his ears to hear car doors slam and people yelling. It got quiet again for a minute or two, until he thought he heard more yelling, but he couldn't be sure. Pretty soon the truck doors slammed again before the driver revved his engine, spun around, and disappeared—pretty much at the same time that Grandma called to him from the back porch.

"Christopher!" she called. "Time to come in!"

For a moment he thought about hiding out in the barn with Magic. But it was getting a little chilly out here, and he wanted to be inside. So he headed for the back porch, still wondering why Troy Vanderveen would have driven out to Uncle Pete's place at this time of night.

Chapter Fifteen

Pete usually didn't mind getting an early start—that was the farmer's life, after all, and he'd been used to getting up early most of his life. But this was ridiculous. He groaned and rolled over when he checked the clock.

"Three in the morning," he whispered, and then wondered what had awakened him in the first place as he felt Dana's cold pillow.

"Dana?" He sat up straight this time, noticing a dim light shining in the kitchen of their little house. He flipped his sheets aside and padded out to investigate, shivering in the early Thursday morning cold.

Dana huddled in her fuzzy bathrobe at the kitchen table, hunched over her laptop and drinking a glass of juice. At first she didn't even notice him standing there next to the table but just kept pecking away at the keys. Maybe that was what had woken him up.

"Honey?" He tried again. "What are you doing out here?"

Dana jumped and gasped at his words, nearly spilling her juice. She took a moment to compose herself.

"Oh! You scared me half to death! I couldn't sleep and was just getting caught up on a little . . . Sorry, I didn't want to wake you up too."

"I don't think you did. How long have you been up?"

"Oh, I don't know. An hour maybe. I woke up around two or two thirty, and I just had all these things from work rolling around in my mind. I figured I might as well get something done so when I have to lead that meeting tomorrow, I'll know what I'm talking about."

Pete yawned and scratched his back. "You mean that meeting *today*, right?"

Dana looked at her watch, as if realizing for the first time what time it was and how soon the rest of the world would be waking up.

"Oh, right. I'm sorry. But I'm almost done here with this agenda. I'll be back to bed in a couple of minutes."

A couple of minutes seemed to mean different things to her these days.

"Is this how it's going to be with the new job?" He mumbled the words and couldn't keep his eyes open. "Home late and up all night?"

"I'm not up all night. I'm just a little . . . you know, wound up about things."

"I'll say."

"But it's just until I get used to it. It's like it was my first year of teaching. It took me twice as long to prepare as it does now. You'll see."

"I thought you said they would add more to the job in the fall if you get the job permanently."

"Did I? Well, don't worry about that. You should get back to sleep. You've been working so hard lately."

"Me? I'm not the one who's waking up at night." Pete didn't argue with her. He could barely keep his eyes open, and Dana had already returned to her typing. He had no idea how her fingers could move so fast over the keyboard, especially not at this time in the morning, and while she was looking in an entirely different direction.

Never mind. He returned to bed, sleepy but for some strange reason unable to sleep, tossing and turning until the alarm really did go off at five thirty. By that time Dana was up and making coffee; its aroma helped pull him out of bed once more but didn't prepare him to be quite as chipper as his wife, who looked showered and well-dressed in a tailored navy-blue skirt and white blouse.

"I never heard you taking a shower," he told her. He must have dozed off without knowing it.

"Here you are." She smiled at him and poured him a cup of coffee. Scrambled eggs sizzled on the stove, and a piece of bread popped out of the toaster. "I made you some breakfast too. Ready to face the day?"

He scratched the stubble on his chin and blinked at her, wondering if maybe he should slip back to bed and try to sleep again. Apparently his wife had confused the notions of night and day and hadn't told him she was going to give up sleeping.

"No, but I guess you are. Ready, I mean." He sounded hoarse but accepted the coffee and her kiss. At this point anything would probably help. But she was already heading for the door with her little leather briefcase tucked under her arm, the one her father had given her when she started teaching. It even had her old initials monogrammed on the front, right under the brass latch: DAS for

Dana Ann Simons. Except now they stood for Dana Ann *Stevenson*. Good thing the initials of her married name hadn't changed.

"I thought I'd get there a little early and get some copies run off," she told him. "I want to be ready."

"Yeah, but five thirty? That's a lot of ready."

She stopped at the open front door, letting in the cold air.

"Come on, farmer boy. Your dad's probably out on his tractor by this time."

"Not all the fields are quite ready yet."

"But some are. I thought you're the one who's supposed to be out and about this time of the morning."

"That's assuming I got any sleep the night before. All bets are off if my beauty rest is interrupted at 3:00 AM."

She smiled as she started to close the front door behind her.

"Sorry about that, handsome. See you later."

The door closed, and Pete stood alone in the middle of the cold kitchen, shivering and not yet dressed. The smell of burning eggs finally woke him more than anything else.

"Yeah," he said to himself. "See you later. But how much later?"

As he was leaving the house a half hour later he checked to make sure he had another pizza in the freezer. He wouldn't admit it to her, but he was getting sick of frozen pizza.

He told himself he would try not to whine about it. He had plenty of other things to worry about. Dad was concerned about cleaning out some of the crop bins to get ready for this season, plus he was annoyed with Pete for spending so much time at the building site. If only he could be in two places at once. He let his mind wander from chore to chore, making a mental to-do list as he drove. Let's see, some of his chores today would be for the farm and some for his house-building, but mostly for his house-building.

Actually, living in town wasn't the worst thing in the world. Driving to and from the farm gave him time to sort things out in his mind, maybe even do a little praying. It seemed he needed a lot of both lately.

Twenty minutes later he pulled up to the construction site, and for a moment he wondered if maybe he was still dreaming.

He stepped out of his old truck into the chilly air over to where the delivery guys had carefully stacked twenty-two windows the other day. Well, they were still stacked just as the boys had left them. But overnight someone had taken nasty black spray paint and scrawled faces and undecipherable writing on twelve of the windows on the top of each stack, as well as all across the side of a backhoe. What the heck? He ran a fingernail over some of the graffiti, just to be sure it didn't come off. No such luck.

"Unbelievable." He shook his head and blinked his eyes. "Absolutely unbelievable."

He'd heard of work sites in some of the bigger cities having problems with vandals and theft, and that hadn't surprised him. But nothing like this ever happened in a place like Bedford, especially not out here at Heather Creek Farm. Who would go to the trouble to ruin all his expensive double-hung windows? He was still standing there, stunned, when his crew rolled up for the morning.

"What's up, boss?" asked his lead framer, Gus Winston, stepping out of his pickup. Pete didn't have to explain. The kid nearly dropped his morning cup of coffee when he saw what Pete was looking at.

"Holy moly." Gus whistled through his teeth and stared. Soon all three of his workers had gathered around the crime scene, and Gus was trying to rub off the worst of the paint with a rag soaked in paint thinner—without much luck.

"I think we should leave it alone," said the youngest in the crew, a bumbling eighteen-year-old kid with wild black hair called Buddy. "We should wait for the CSI guys to get here."

Pete knew there weren't going to be any crime scene investigators in this neck of the woods, not like the ones on TV. He pulled out his cell phone but then realized he hadn't charged it, so he had to borrow Gus's phone to call the county sheriff's department. His hand was actually shaking as he punched in the number. Because one thing was sure: Whoever did this was not going to get away with it.

And then the thought occurred to him. *What if...*

No, it was just too crazy. He couldn't imagine Walt would ever do such a thing. But then he couldn't imagine Walt threatening to sue him either.

Who else had a motive like Walt? What if he was trying to bully Pete into stopping work, and making it look like the work of teenage vandals?

Stranger things had happened.

A couple of hours later deputy Abe Johnson showed up in his patrol car to take a report, and they all took a break to gather around the ruined windows once more. Pete had already done a bit of mental math on the damage. Twelve top-of-the-line vinyl, double-hung windows at $226 apiece would bring it to around $2,700. Plus damage to his backhoe. And it all came out of his pocket.

"Look at this." Buddy pointed to the dirt next to the windows. "There's footprints right here. We could take some plaster casts, and then ... well, you know how they do that sort of thing. I read about it once in one of those detective books."

Abe gave him a sideways glance, looking both puzzled and amused.

"We don't do plaster casts, Buddy," he said. "And those are probably your own boot prints."

Gus harrumphed as Pete stood watching, arms crossed.

"Well, I still want to press charges," said Pete, and his crew nodded their agreement. "That is, assuming we can find out who to press charges against."

Pete wasn't about to voice his suspicions—not yet. Abe nodded his understanding and stood up to his full six feet five inches as he scribbled a couple of notes in his notebook, including the value of the ruined windows. Then— and perhaps to satisfy the young crime-show fans—he pulled a digital camera out of his patrol car and snapped a couple of shots.

"I think I know who did this, by the way," Abe told them, and he seemed to enjoy holding their full attention for a quiet moment. "Kids over at the high school. A little gang of troublemakers, wannabe tough guys. Been in trouble for doing the same thing in town. Same kind of dumb little painted faces. Same kind of markings."

"You'd think they would change it up or something," said Gus, pulling out his thinner-soaked rag again. "Seems pretty stupid to me."

"Yeah, stupid criminals." Buddy's laugh seemed a little out of place. "I was watching one of those shows last night called *Stupid Criminals*, and they had this guy robbing a convenience store, but then he looked straight at the camera, and . . ."

His voice trailed off when he finally noticed the deputy frowning at him.

"Guess you had to be there," he said in a much softer voice.

"You really think you know?" Pete didn't mind setting aside his earlier suspicions. And he had no idea it was going to be so easy. No plaster casts, no DNA testing, none of that CSI or reality-TV stuff. "Then what do we do?"

"We may not be able to prove anything, but I'll go pay 'em a visit." He turned to Pete and handed him his card. "My guess is that they'll deny everything, just like they always do, and maybe there won't be much we can do about it unless somebody talks, or unless somebody saw 'em do it. But, Pete . . ."

He paused, looking around at the house, now nearly framed. Next would come the roof sheathing, and after that shingles and exterior siding. If it wasn't for the windows here, it would actually be looking pretty good.

"I heard you were going to have to relocate the whole

thing anyway," said the deputy. "Surprised you're going ahead with it on the same spot."

"Oh, that." Pete jammed his hands in the pockets of his jeans. Apparently word about his little border dispute with Walt was getting around. "We're going to get it worked out. I'm just waiting on a call from the planning office to confirm things."

"Hmm. Not what I heard down at the courthouse. But for your sake, I hope you're right. I'd hate to see you have to tear it down and do all this work over again."

"Who said anything about tearing it down?" Buddy looked confused. "I'm not tearing it down."

Gus calmed him down, assuring him that nothing was going to be torn down.

"And now these windows," added the deputy. He shook his head and frowned at the mess. "Anyway, if you find out anything new from this end, don't hesitate to give me a call."

Pete would do that. He thought of calling Dana to tell her what had happened but then changed his mind when he remembered she would probably be in one of her big meetings by this time.

He really needed to follow up with the planning office. Meanwhile, there was no reason to slow the work. Dana would have her house right here on their land, Walt Freeman or no Walt Freeman.

Chapter Sixteen

S am Slater!"

Sam froze for a moment in the school hallway when he heard Mr. Santos call his name. What would happen if he pretended not to hear and just kept walking to his next class? Too late for that. Jake—who was walking next to him—had already said, "Oooo, busted!" loud enough for everyone around them to hear.

He tried to look like a busy student who had to get to class right away.

"Hey, Mr. Santos." Sam tried to smile as he kind of shuffled along sideways. "How are you doing?"

Mr. Santos just crooked a finger and motioned Sam to join him in his office. There was no escape. Sam slipped inside and tried to hover by the door, but Mr. Santos pointed him toward a chair by his desk before he shut the door behind them.

"Actually, Mr. Santos," Sam tried to explain, "I'm going to be late for sociology."

Mr. Santos had that covered. He raised a finger as he got on his phone and punched a couple of numbers.

"Mr. Anderson?" he said. "Jeff Santos here. I'm having a chat with Sam Slater that's going to take a couple more minutes. Just so you know, all right? Good. Thanks."

He hung up the phone just as someone else knocked on his door. Mr. Duncan stepped inside and then stood against the closed door with his arms crossed. Like Mr. Santos had it timed. Like some kind of sting operation.

Oh, man. Sam bit his lip. *It doesn't get any worse than this.*

"I see you finally caught up to him," said Mr. Duncan, and Mr. Santos nodded, the two of them acting like tag-team heavies. The counselor nodded his head and leaned forward.

"You know why we needed to talk to you, don't you?" Mr. Santos said.

Sam swallowed hard and tried to play dumb as he shrugged his shoulders, but of course he knew.

"I just want to know if there's some kind of problem here," he told Sam, "or if it's just plain procrastination."

"Uh . . ." Sam wasn't sure how to answer. Neither option sounded good, although probably both were true.

"Look, Sam." Mr. Duncan cleared his throat. "You're a smart kid, and we just want to help. You *do* intend to graduate, don't you?"

Sam shrugged again and slumped down a little more in the uncomfortable vinyl chair. If he could have hidden underneath it, he would have. Instead, he mumbled, "I guess so."

"You guess so?" Now Mr. Santos rubbed the side of his head like he had a bad headache. "I need to tell you something then. We've talked about this, and Mr. Duncan is prepared to withhold your diploma until we see a completed senior project with a completed report. I don't know how to say it more plainly than that."

"Yeah, I know." Sam tried desperately to get them off his back. "I've had some ideas, but..."

His voice trailed off, and Mr. Santos took up the slack again.

"Is there a reason you've put it off this long?" He wanted an answer Sam couldn't give. How could Sam explain that avoiding the project was the only way he could think of to hold back the future? Unfortunately it wasn't working.

Sam could only shake his head no.

"All right." Finally Mr. Santos's expression seemed to soften a little. "Then let's not make this harder than it should be. No more putting it off. Promise me now that you'll get this turned in by the end of the month, okay? That's two weeks from now."

"Sure." By this time Sam would have promised them nearly anything, just to get out of there. He took his cue to stand up. Mr. Duncan didn't uncross his arms, but he did step away from the door so Sam could escape.

"By the end of the month, remember!" Parting words from the school counselor.

"Got it." Sam never thought getting to sociology class sounded so good. But he still had no idea what he was going to do for the project—and the future—he couldn't seem to avoid.

Chapter
Seventeen

Pete rolled over and pulled the covers to his chin.

"Wake up, honey," Dana said, her soft voice interrupting his dreams. "You've got to see this."

He didn't answer. It had been a long Thursday, and the week wasn't over yet.

"Please," she insisted, tugging on his elbow now. "Just for a minute."

With some amount of righteous moaning he forced his eyelids open to see one of those late-night home shows. People really had time to watch that stuff? Well, apparently his wife did. A quick glance at his bedside alarm showed it was nearly midnight.

"What are you doing up anyway?" he asked.

"Just trying to get my mind off everything at school today. But look at the wraparound porch they're showing, Pete. It's perfect! Can't you imagine sitting out on the porch after work on a summer day, rocking in your chair, watching the kids play?"

He nearly threw off his covers as he sat bolt upright.

"Hold on, hold on. Is that some kind of announcement? What kids are we talking about? Don't tell me you're already—"

For a moment Dana looked at him in confusion, and then she burst out laughing.

"No, silly. I'm not pregnant. I'm just saying that when we do have kids, we need a wraparound porch, like the one on this show. That's all. You're funny."

Pete sighed and settled back into his pillow.

"Don't scare me like that. That's not a good thing to joke around about in the middle of the night."

"But what about that porch? You can add it to the plans, can't you?"

"It would poke out even more. We're already close to the property line as is."

"But not *over* the property line, right? You told me that was all taken care of with the neighbor."

Pete sighed. Not again and not now.

"I'm just saying you can't just tack on a porch at this stage. We'd have to redo the trusses and add to the foundation, not to mention adding a lot more roofing."

"But it could be done?"

"Theoretically. For a whole lot more time and money. But on top of what we've lost from the vandalism, no way it's in the budget."

Dana didn't sound as if she was going to give up that easily.

"But our budget was based on what I was making when I was just a teacher. Assistant principal gets a lot more salary, you know."

"I thought you're not officially the assistant principal yet. Just the *acting* assistant principal."

"Well, yes. But Chad said I should apply."

So now it was *Chad* and not Mr. Duncan. Hmm.

"OK, well once we start getting assistant-principal pay-checks, maybe we can talk about a new budget. Until then I have to stick to the old one."

The home show switched to a commercial with a very loud man hawking a magic cleanser guaranteed to work or your money cheerfully refunded.

"But if we wait," said Dana, her voice rising to match the TV pitchman's, "it's going to be too late. Don't you think the porch looks good?"

"Looks great," he mumbled. "Ain't gonna happen."

"But if money isn't the issue," she asked, "what is?"

"You say money isn't the issue. I say it still is. And we're just too far along in the process to make a major change like this. And that's all I have to say about it at midnight."

At that point he tried to roll over on his side, away from the argument.

"Wait a minute," she held him back. "You can't just roll over and say the case is closed. I still think we should try to do this. You said yourself you like the idea."

"You can't just see something on TV and say you want it, and boom, expect it to happen." He raised his voice more than he intended. "Now just forget about it and get some sleep, would you?"

Dana didn't answer right away. She snapped off the TV, and Pete thought the matter was settled—until he heard a quiet sniffling from the other side of the bed. He sighed and rolled back over to face her.

"You're not crying, are you?" he asked.

"If I were, you wouldn't care."

Uh-oh. Pete backtracked in his mind. Was she upset because he'd explained to her the expense of radically altering their house plans at this stage? She didn't understand what it would take to make big changes at this stage of construction.

Besides, what was wrong with the nice little front porch they'd already designed and agreed on? It looked a lot like the back porch at his folks' house. Didn't that count for anything?

And what was the use of staying up so late anyway? He thought maybe her exhaustion made her say and do things she really didn't mean. She hadn't been like this before they were married. Clearly, he still had a long way to go before he understood women. He slipped out of bed and returned with a peace offering in the form of a handful of tissues. She accepted them without a word.

"You're welcome," he told her, but that was the end of their so-called conversation.

Pete lay back down and closed his eyes but could not reclaim his dreams or his sleep. *How old is this lumpy old mattress anyway?* He wondered. *And who put the rocks in my pillow?*

He lay awake, very much alone in his thoughts, wondering what it would actually take to add Dana's wraparound porch. Later the blueprints had etched themselves in his mind, along with the new price and materials lists and revised work schedules. And then he began on a list of to-dos. Would he really have to order new roof trusses? How far out of the water would it blow the already inflated budget? What about his workers?

By 2:00 AM he had a list of questions as long as his arm,

but zero answers. Meanwhile, the sound of regular breathing told him that Dana finally slept soundly beside him, unaware of his problems.

Stupid home show! He wanted to take that cursed remote and throw it right through the TV.

PETE THOUGHT ABOUT bringing up the porch issue the next morning, just to clear the air, but Dana didn't stop to catch her breath as she rushed about that morning— from blow-drying her hair and dressing in her nice clothes to putting on makeup and popping in her contacts. On her way past the kitchen she grabbed a piece of toast and sipped a cup of coffee. He didn't dare mention that her eyes looked a little puffy.

"Look," he said as she paused by the door, "about last night . . ."

She stopped him with a raised hand.

"It doesn't matter," she said. "And I'm going to be late."

He didn't believe her for a second, except that when he looked at his watch he nearly choked on his coffee.

"Talk about late! I told my guys to show up a few minutes early today, and here it is—"

Dana left him to worry about his own tardiness, mentioning something about being home by five or five thirty. Good enough. As she hurried out the door he rushed back to the bedroom to throw on some jeans and a flannel work shirt. But as Dana drove down their little driveway and turned onto Oldham Street, he couldn't help thinking the honeymoon was over.

HE THOUGHT ABOUT IT all that day, working with his framers for a couple of hours early on and then rushing over to the barn to help his dad work on a seeder that needed adjusting. He managed to break away midafternoon to check back on the house, where the regular *ka-tap-tap-tap* of air hammers told him the welcome news that at least somebody was getting some work done.

"Me?" he answered Buddy's "How ya doin'?" question before even thinking about it. "I feel like a chicken with its head cut off."

"Yeah, I know the feeling," Buddy replied, leaning against a newly framed wall. "Last year my girlfriend started making me lists of things to do around her apartment. You know, like fix the faucet that was dripping and the fan in the bathroom, that kind of thing? It was "honey do this" and "honey do that." Drove me crazy."

Pete untied his tool belt and tossed it aside, knowing he could easily work a couple more hours. Dana probably wouldn't be home until five or six anyway. Maybe later. Even so . . .

"I'm taking off a little early," he yelled to Buddy and Gus. Buddy looked at him with his gap-toothed smile.

"Hot date, huh?"

"I've got a honey-do list of my own."

He didn't stick around to explain or enjoy Buddy's slack-jawed look of *huh?* Instead he hurried home to make sure he got there before Dana. This would have to be good.

Later, standing in the kitchen, the only question was, what could he cook that would impress his bride and soften her up after last night's argument? He rifled through the small pantry, looking for good ideas.

"Aha!" He held up the box in the light. Well, the picture on the front looked pretty good. How hard could Hamburger Helper lasagna be?

Not very, as it turned out. He wasn't sure how much hamburger was in the package he found in the freezer, but he managed to brown it pretty well. The noodles and sauce went in OK too, plus the added spices he discovered in Dana's spice cabinet. "Hmm..." he mused, sprinkling in another spice. "Oregano sounds Italian, doesn't it?"

A little buttered toast went in the oven to warm while he opened a can of green beans and heated them on the stovetop next to the simmering lasagna. Meanwhile, he found a nice tablecloth for the dining room table. He lit some candles and then set out two of the nice wine glasses they'd received as a wedding gift. A handful of bright yellow daffodils from outside next to the sidewalk would add a splash of color, and a little low music on the stereo would add to the atmosphere.

There we go. He smiled to himself. Dana was going to love this romantic dinner surprise.

Only problem was, five o'clock came and went, and so did five thirty. In the rush this morning, hadn't she mentioned she'd be home by five thirty? At a quarter to six he slipped outside to clip a couple more flowers just as Dana pulled up next to his old truck. Feeling like a little boy with his first crush, he guarded the front door with the little bouquet hidden behind his back.

"Welcome to your castle," he told her as she trudged up the little walk. Though her face looked drawn and beaten, she actually did manage a smile as he presented her with the flowers.

"That's so sweet," she managed in a hoarse whisper. He took her briefcase and opened the door with a grand, sweeping gesture.

"And welcome to Café Stevenson."

He took her purse and briefcase, pulled out the chair with a flourish, and invited her to have a seat and wait to be served. Then he scurried back into the kitchen.

"What are you doing in there?" she asked. "I hear a lot of pots and pans clattering."

"Not to worry, madam. Your entrée will be out momentarily."

The lasagna was actually still steaming when he brought it out, very well-done and not really looking anything like the picture on the package. But what it lacked in looks, it would make up for in taste, Pete thought confidently.

"Your din-NAIR," he said, setting the plate in front of her with another flourish and a fake French accent. This was supposed to be an Italian meal, but since he wasn't sure how to do an Italian accent, he settled for French as he poured a spot of sparkling apple juice in her wine glass.

"You would like to sample the vintage, oui?"

Dana giggled and played along with him, swirling the juice in her glass and giving it a sniff before nodding.

"It's wonderful," she told him.

And the main course? Maybe a little chewy, and maybe a little too much salt. But overall . . .

"Not bad." Dana hurried a swig of juice and took a bite. She cleared her throat and smiled weakly. She wasn't fooling him.

"But maybe you want to cook it next time?" He finished the sentence for her, and she burst out laughing.

"I kind of had a clue when I smelled it," she told him, lowering her fork. "Did you follow the directions?"

"Actually, I..." He pushed his plate aside. "I'm sorry. I ruined it. Just like I ruin a lot of other things."

"No, you didn't." She looked at him with a soft smile and a sparkle in her eyes. "I throw some crazy idea at you in the middle of the night and expect you to jump through hoops. It's my fault."

"No, it's not." He reached under the tablecloth for a folder he had stashed there. "It was a good idea. Here. Look."

She leaned forward to see the rough sketch he'd made earlier in the day.

"I figured we could add on something freestanding and cover it with something like awnings." He pointed out the porch sketch and the materials list. "Here, see..."

She looked at him instead, leaning closer for a welcome kiss.

"You need a little practice in the cooking department, my dear," she told him, tears of a different kind now filling her eyes. "But I'm sure glad I married you."

Chapter
Eighteen

Saturday morning found Charlotte "in the zone," dusting and vacuuming and doing the week's wash. Sometimes, it seemed, all at the same time. She hummed a praise song they'd been learning in church over the past several weeks—an old favorite, really: "Amazing Grace," but with some added lyrics about chains and being set free, or something like that.

Well, her chains might be gone, but as she pushed her vacuum around Charlotte imagined herself still attached by a power cord.

"Charlotte!"

The shout spun her around from where she was vacuuming the living room. Goodness! Her heart settled when she saw Dana standing in the kitchen, and she quickly snapped off the machine.

"I'm terribly sorry," she told her daughter-in-law as the machine wound itself down. "I didn't hear you over the noise."

"I know." Dana smiled in that appealing way of hers as their voices returned to normal. "I didn't mean to startle you. When I get to vacuuming I sort of zone out too."

"Well, it's good to see you. You'll have some coffee?"

Charlotte left the vacuum standing in the living room and stepped into the kitchen to see if she had any coffee left. For good measure she pulled out a Tupperware container of oatmeal-chocolate chip cookies, as well.

"I really shouldn't," Dana said as she accepted a green John Deere mug and held it out as Charlotte filled it for her. "But a little chocolate in the morning sounds perfect, actually."

"How's your new job?" asked Charlotte. "I hear bits and snippets from Pete, but you know how men are. You practically have to pry it out of him."

"I suppose you're right." Dana smiled and paused. "And actually, that's part of what I wanted to talk to you about."

"You mean men? Honey, believe me, they're not too hard to figure out. And I'm sure you know more about Pete by now than I'll ever know. Or want to."

"Well, I don't know about that. You've known him all his life."

"But you're catching up."

Charlotte studied the young woman. She looked casual and comfy in jeans and a red U of N sweatshirt, her dark hair pulled back into a ponytail. But Charlotte could see that something was nagging at Dana; that much was obvious from the hint of pain in her eyes. What could be wrong? Charlotte helped herself to a cookie and waited.

"I suppose I am. Actually, I was wondering if I could ask you something. Uh, you once wanted to be a nurse, didn't you?"

"A nurse, yes." Charlotte smiled at the distant memory. "But that was years ago—before I met Bob."

"Had you thought of being a nurse for a long time?"

"You could say that. I was in the seventh or eighth grade, and I read a biography of Florence Nightingale. From that time on, all I could think of was being a nurse, just like her."

"What changed? What happened?"

"Oh, I don't know. I met Bob, for one thing, and he was destined to be a farmer, no two ways about it. And I was in love, so that made the decision a little easier. If I wanted to be with him, I would have to build a life right here on this farm."

"But couldn't you still have been a nurse too?"

Charlotte shook her head slowly.

"I suppose, theoretically. But we both decided we would work at this together and not lead such separate lives, the way . . . some people do these days. I'm not talking about you, you understand. I just—"

"Oh, I didn't take it that way."

Charlotte talked through what could have been an awkward silence.

"Besides, we both very much wanted to have a family, and I wanted to spend time with the kids. I guess I'm old-fashioned that way."

Dana seemed to chew on that for a few moments. Was that not what she had wanted to hear? Young women of her generation had different views. And Charlotte certainly didn't want to offend her.

"I don't mean to be dispensing unwelcome advice," she told Dana. But that only prompted a vigorous response as Dana shook her head.

"Not at all. I asked, didn't I?"

Now she smiled, but Charlotte could tell something was still bothering her as she went on.

"I was just wondering, though, did you ever think you missed out on anything? Was it hard to lay aside your dreams when you married a farmer? Not that it's bad marrying a farmer, obviously. I mean, look who I just married."

They both had a good laugh at that. Charlotte nibbled on her cookie, still wondering what Dana was getting at.

"I guess it never occurred to me that I was missing out on anything," Charlotte finally admitted, swirling her coffee and adding a touch more sweetener. "Laying my dreams aside? Not really. I've never regretted my life. Although sometimes I wonder why things happened the way they did, you know, with Denise and all."

"I didn't mean to bring up a touchy subject."

"No, no. I've never claimed to have a perfect life. But that's where faith comes in, and it's certainly never been boring. Things turn out. In fact, I'll tell you something I've never shared with anyone but Bob."

That got Dana's attention. She gripped her mug with two hands and leaned forward expectantly.

"Well, you know I told everyone I was going to be a nurse, right? All my girlfriends were expecting it throughout my teen years. In fact, some of them even jokingly called me Nurse Charlotte."

"Well, come to think of it, you do look like a nurse."

"Ha! But then I found out in eleventh-grade biology class that I had a major problem with blood. We saw these films, you know, on the different systems of the body, and whenever it got to anything about blood, I started to feel light-headed. I didn't tell anyone, but I nearly fainted. And then when we had to dissect a fetal pig I had to excuse myself more than once. I was ill in the ladies' room."

"You? Squeamish?" Dana chuckled. "I would have never believed it. Pete's told me stories of how you always had to patch him up every time he skinned his knee or cut himself. There was the time he tried to crawl over a barbed wire fence, right?"

"Oh, yes. Fifteen stitches on his leg. Blood all over the kitchen floor, right here."

She pointed at the floor next to the sink, and in her mind's eye she could still see ten-year-old Pete's panic as she tried to calm him down and patch him up. The little boy had thought he was going to die, poor thing.

"And you weren't squeamish about that?" Dana wondered. Charlotte shook her head.

"Not when it was my own child. I suppose my mothering instincts kicked in; I knew I had to be the adult and take care of things."

"Hmm." Dana seemed to take it all in, and Charlotte wondered what else was on her mind as the younger woman sat and stirred her coffee. She let Dana take her own time to consider whatever was really bothering her. Finally she took a deep breath and blurted out her announcement:

"I'm really enjoying the assistant principal position, but—" She winced as if expecting a negative reaction. "It's turning out to be a big time commitment."

"More than you expected?" Charlotte asked quietly, her head tilted as if to hear better.

"I'm not sure what I expected. I have to say I do really enjoy the challenge and being able to make big decisions. That part I enjoy a lot. And the pay raise is going to be very nice. We're going to be able to buy a few things we hadn't counted on, and I hope maybe even make the house a little nicer. It's just that . . ."

Again she sighed, searching for words.

"It's just that we—Pete and I—we've been arguing a lot more than I expected. Almost every night this week. I get home late from meetings, and he's sitting home alone in the dark, eating frozen pizza or something else that's just as disgusting. I hate it. We're supposed to be happy newlyweds, and now this job comes up, and it sort of takes over everything."

"But that could change, right? Once you get used to the job?"

"That's just it. Principal Duncan is passing along so many responsibilities—and I don't blame him for that—but this is just the beginning. There's a lot of stress."

Charlotte nodded. Her coffee was getting cold, but she took another sip anyway.

"I would guess maybe it's not as serious as you think," she told Dana. "And you know what they say about the first few months of marriage."

"No. What do they say?"

Charlotte felt a twinge of embarrassment for having mentioned it, but now that she had brought it up she might as well spill it.

"Well, I don't know *exactly* what they say. For me, though? All I really remember about that first year was lots of frustration and tears."

"Really?" Dana seemed surprised. "You?"

"Are you kidding? Just about every other day Bob would say something, or not say something, or do something, or not do something, and I would misunderstand, or my feelings would be hurt, or some such silly thing. There was a lot of adjustment—on both our parts. I suspect you might know what I mean."

Dana smiled again and sampled another cookie.

"And you two turned out OK," she told Charlotte.

"Well!" Charlotte couldn't keep from chuckling. "I suppose we've just learned to be a little more patient, and to give each other a break once in a while. A little grace, I mean."

"Amazing grace." Dana echoed the words.

Charlotte hadn't meant to offer a sermon; it just came out that way.

"Of course, I don't know what that has to do with your job situation exactly. But I'm sure you'll do what's best. And as far as your marriage goes, you can relax in the fact that everyone struggles a little at first. It's not easy. But I do know that Pete loves you very much. And he's committed to you."

Dana nodded and stared out the window in the direction of the house Pete was building for them. She hadn't mentioned any stresses or strains from that project, but Charlotte could imagine there were plenty. Couples often clashed over such things, even relatively happy newlyweds. Speaking of which . . .

"Hey!" Pete boomed out as he stepped through the back door and into the kitchen. "Look who's here."

He paused in the doorway as he looked at his wife, shaking his head so that sawdust rained down on the kitchen floor. As she rose to her feet, that reminded Charlotte of

the twenty-five other things on her Saturday chores list—
including the rest of the vacuuming.

"We were just having some cookies, Pete." She pointed
at the Tupperware container from which she had already
removed more than her share of cookies. "Please help yourself. I still have a few things to do this morning. I should
go."

"Charlotte." Dana caught her by the hand. "Thank you.
That means a lot to me, what you said."

"It was nothing." Charlotte squeezed her daughter-in-
law's hand in return. "But you should feel free to stop by
anytime."

Pete looked from Dana to his mom and back again, and
of course he had no idea what they were talking about.
Even so, Charlotte thought she could see a hint of the same
dark cloud in his expression that she had seen in Dana's.

"Well, I was just taking a break, and . . ." He nodded at
Dana. "And now I'm glad to see you here so we can take a
moment to relax together."

Charlotte assumed that Pete was probably wishing his
mom wasn't in the room; Dana found him a mug and they
sat down together.

"I was just leaving," Charlotte announced as she
returned to her chores. Then that new song from church
came to mind once again. She couldn't remember all the
words, but she did recall that they promised mercy.

They could certainly use a little mercy, a little grace.

Chapter
Nineteen

Sure enough, at church the next morning they sang "Amazing Grace" again—the one with the added words. Charlotte thought it was just like God to remind her.

As she pondered the meaning of the lyrics, she got the clear impression there was more than one way to apply those words—especially when Emily skipped up to her right after the service while everyone was milling about in the foyer for coffee and fellowship time.

"Grandma, is it okay if me and some friends hang out this afternoon?"

"You mean some friends and I," Charlotte corrected her. "And which friends are we talking about?"

"Oh, you know. Just kids from school. Ashley. A couple of others. Depends."

What exactly it depended on, Charlotte wasn't sure. But still she needed to know a little more than just "we're hanging out" and "depends."

"We're having your birthday dinner tonight, don't forget. You'd need to be home no later than five."

"But Troy was going to take me out for dessert."

"Not on your birthday, Emily," Charlotte replied. "That's reserved for family. Besides, you know you need to ask permission before you go out on a date."

"Oh, Grandma," Emily sighed.

"Rules are rules, Emily. You can go with your friends, but I'd like you home at four thirty. And if you're late your Uncle Pete will eat all your cake and ice cream too."

"You're just kidding me, Grandma. You haven't made me any cake."

"Not yet, I haven't. But I will. And remember, four thirty, not a minute later."

"But Grandma," Emily pressed, "what will I tell Troy?" Charlotte stopped for a moment as she saw her daughter's eyes staring at her from her granddaughter's face.

Charlotte shook her head to bring herself back to the present. "Well . . . he's welcome to join us for your birthday dinner if he likes."

This time Emily stared at her with wide eyes.

"Troy? You can't be serious."

"I'm serious. Ask him. Unless you don't want him to come, of course."

"No, it's not that. I'm just shocked you would offer."

"Ask him or don't ask him." Charlotte pointed to the entry. "We'll have plenty of food either way. But it looks as if your friends are waiting for you."

Emily looked toward where the other girls waved to her.

"Right," she said. "I'd better go. Four thirty."

With that she hurried through the crowd to the front doors.

"Emily, wait just a minute," Charlotte called after her

with one last thought, but it was too late. "You never told me who's driving. Anyone I know?"

Perhaps Emily just didn't hear her above the buzz of the after-church crowd. In any case, she skipped away as if she hadn't. A moment later the front double doors slammed shut, leaving Charlotte holding her steaming cup of coffee and unanswered questions.

She blinked her eyes shut in a quick prayer. *Did I do the right thing, Lord? I don't want to make the same mistakes I made with Denise.*

Charlotte prayed quietly for just a moment, standing alone on the fringe of the Sunday crowd.

I'm trying to show Emily more mercy. I hope this is the right way to do it.

"Where's Emily going?" asked Christopher, coming up beside his grandmother as he munched on a glazed doughnut.

"Apparently she's just going out with some friends. You only took one of those doughnuts, didn't you?"

"Sure, Grandma." Christopher nodded his head. "But I forgot to ask: Dylan asked me to come over to his house this afternoon. He got a new hockey game he wants me to help him break in."

"Oh, really?" Charlotte looked at him to make sure. "You mean a video hockey game, right?"

Christopher gave her a puzzled look.

"What other kind of game is there?"

She could have laughed but instead gave Christopher the same warning about being done by four thirty, so no one would miss Emily's birthday dinner.

"I suppose we could drop you off on the way out of town," she added.

"Thanks, Grandma!" He caught sight of another boy his age from Sunday school, who ran past with a doughnut clutched in each hand.

"Just one." Charlotte reminded Christopher as he ran down the hallway to follow the boy. He stopped and turned back to face Charlotte.

"I forgot to tell you!" he yelled back. Charlotte wished he would just walk up to her and speak in a normal voice instead of announcing it to the entire church. But that was a twelve-year-old boy for you. "Sam said to say he was hanging out with Paul this afternoon and he'll be home later."

With that he turned back around and disappeared down the hall, just as Melody Givens stepped up with an amused smile.

"At least they're busy," said Melody, balancing a small plate of doughnut holes and a cup of coffee. "You wouldn't want them to be bored, would you?"

"I suppose not," answered Charlotte. "Although it would be nice if they all made it home for dinner."

"Ah, now you know what I face every day, my friend." Melody dispatched one of the doughnut holes, put down her coffee cup, and adjusted a bright daisy clip in her perky hairdo. Not many women her age—somewhere in her mid-thirties—could get away with that kind of fashion state-ment. But the sun always shone on Melody Givens.

"I make a special at the restaurant," she went on, "and what do you bet no one orders it?"

"Oh, I don't know, Melody. I can't imagine."

"No? Happened just last week when I made zucchini and rice soup. Thought it would be a great idea. You should have tasted the recipe. Sounds strange, but believe me, it was to die for! And how many people do you think were brave enough to order it? Even after I talked it up with everyone who came in and made it the special of the day."

"I don't know, Melody. It sounds very good to—"

"Not one." Melody put her thumb and forefinger together in a big 0. "Zero. Zilch. All the kids ever want is a burger and fries with a Coke, their folks order meatloaf with gravy, and the grandparents ask for liver and onions. Nothing wrong with that. But why do I bother offering something new? I ask myself."

Charlotte hadn't meant to touch on such a hot button, but it was always nice to have someone like Melody to chat with. Although with the café owner, the conversation often turned to food or recipes or the restaurant. And just the thought of Melody's food could add an inch or two to Charlotte's waistline.

"But enough about me." Melody looked at her with genuine concern. "How are you doing lately? I hear your Emily has a boyfriend."

By this time Emily's friendship with Troy had obviously become common knowledge. Charlotte took another sip of coffee, which was way too strong for her taste.

"Actually, Mel, I thought perhaps I'd ask you about it. I'm . . . I'm not quite sure how I should react to all this. The kids these days seem to relate a little differently than we ever did."

"I know!" Melody's voice rose in agreement. "All I hear about is how they're texting or e-mailing or whatever the latest e-thing happens to be. I'm afraid to ask Ashley because she'll probably just roll her eyes and say, 'Oh, Mom, nobody does that anymore. That's so last year.' "

"And all Emily will tell me is that they're 'hanging out' with a group. There's never anything specific. No specific place, no specific people."

"Unfortunately, it seems to be the status quo."

"When Ashley was dating Ryan, how did you handle things? Did you encourage them at all?"

"Encourage them?" Melody blew out a little exclamation point of powdered sugar before washing it down with another sip of coffee. "Well, I was always polite to the boy, but just between us, I can't say I was thrilled. In fact, I'm really glad they drifted apart during my cancer episode."

"But you didn't say that to her."

"Heavens no. I'm sure she would have rebelled if I'd done that."

"Hmm." Charlotte recognized herself in Melody Givens, especially in her lack of enthusiasm for Emily's budding love interest. So maybe she was taking the right approach by inviting Troy to dinner. She remembered all too well the late-night confrontations with Denise, the heated arguments, the awkward moments. Back then she and Bob had expressed their disapproval in no uncertain terms.

And look where it had gotten them.

By now Charlotte's coffee had cooled off and she held it stiffly so as not to spill the rest. Melody looked sympathetically at Charlotte.

"I know what you're thinking, Charlotte. But teenage crushes come and go. And just because Emily's infatuated with Troy, that doesn't mean she's going to go down the same road as Denise did with Kevin. You know that, don't you?"

Charlotte nodded at her friend's encouragement. "I know that."

"Please don't worry. Just remember that Emily is not Denise. And for that matter, you're not the same person today as you were back then. You're a little older, a little wiser, right?"

"A little older, in any case." They both laughed.

"And I'm here for you whenever you need me."

Melody gave her a hug, being careful not to spill their coffee. By that time the crowd in the foyer had thinned considerably. Over in the corner, Bob was still chatting with a couple of his farmer friends, probably about planting and tractors and such, but he caught her eye and glanced at the doors—his signal to say, *Shouldn't we go now?*

She said her good-byes to everyone and her thank you to Melody, and soon they were riding in Charlotte's little Ford, headed for Dylan Lonetree's house on the other side of town.

"Emily's hanging out with her boyfriend again?" Christopher piped up from the backseat. He knew. Bob nearly drove through a stop sign as he looked up at the rearview mirror.

"Who said anything about boyfriends?" Bob asked. Charlotte patted him on the arm, trying to smooth things over.

"Relax," she told them both. "Nobody said anything about boyfriends. She's just going to be spending the afternoon with Ashley and—"

"And her boyfriend." Christopher finished her sentence.

Charlotte glanced over at Bob and saw his expression darken considerably, and it remained dark all the way to the Lonetrees', where they dropped Christopher off and promised to pick him up later that afternoon.

"She *is* turning sixteen, you know," Charlotte told Bob a few more miles down the road. "And we did tell her she could date when she was sixteen."

But she had to admit that despite Melody's pep talk—or perhaps because of it—she felt just as concerned as her husband looked. What was she supposed to do about it? Neither of them said much more all the way home.

Chapter
Twenty

Charlotte thought about Emily and Troy all afternoon as she busied herself with cleaning and getting the dinner prepared. The house was quiet and the only sounds were Toby whimpering to be let out and Bob snoring during a Sunday afternoon nap in his easy chair.

Once she felt the house was in order, she picked up her prairie romance novel, thinking she might read to distract herself. But she couldn't sit down, and she couldn't stop thinking about what Melody had told her after church.

Teenage crushes come and go.

Of course they did. But sitting there in the too-quiet house felt like sitting on the train tracks, waiting for the wreck to arrive—a handsome train wreck by the name of Troy Vanderveen.

She followed Toby out on the porch to pray, clear her head, and perhaps breathe some fresh air. A band of pregnant, dark clouds had formed to the northwest, bearing down on Adams County and Heather Creek Farm with the promise of more rain, perhaps even a spring storm. In fact, she could smell the distant dampness; so could Toby, who raised her nose to the breeze and sniffed.

"Storm on the way, girl?"

The old dog thumped her tail on the little porch and looked up at Charlotte just as a clap of thunder startled her and made her bark with alarm. Charlotte reached down to pat Toby's head.

"It's OK," she said, gently stroking Toby's ears. "If the storm comes, we'll just go back inside."

They stood and watched for a while as the weather advanced almost as if it had targeted their little farm and was charging straight for them. And as they watched, Charlotte tried to hold back her tumbling storm of thoughts, mixing them haphazardly with prayers and cries for help. What to do? How to do it?

I need more wisdom than I own, Lord, she finally prayed. *Much more.*

The way she saw it, she only had a couple of options—neither of which appealed very much. One, she could have dug in her heels to forbid Emily from seeing an older boy. Perhaps they should have been more explicit before simply saying that yes, she could go out on dates when she was sixteen. Perhaps they should have told her not to date older guys.

But now it was too late, and Charlotte had little difficulty imagining the tsunami that would result if she and Bob decided on that course of action.

"I think that's what they would call the nuclear option," she told Toby. The dog sat down and began scratching, still keeping a wary eye on the advancing clouds.

Her second option would simply be to let it happen. Ruffle the least amount of feathers. Let the storm come and hope it would pass without causing much damage.

Perhaps she could slip in a few words of grandmotherly advice—which Emily would politely deflect. Then she could simply stand back and let the relationship take its course. And maybe Emily would surprise her and show a little maturity. She had certainly grown since coming to the farm.

Toby jumped at the lightning that suddenly forked across the sky just before a much louder crack of thunder reverberated in the air around them. Trees around the farm began to sway and swing in the oncoming wind while a small flock of starlings appeared from behind the barn and retreated before the onslaught. Charlotte and Toby stood on the porch, watching. She could almost hear the rain advancing across their fields, and soon lightning and thunder exploded around them simultaneously, the percussion creating a violent concert that reminded Charlotte of kettle drums and shotgun shells.

Next came a curtain of rain and hail sweeping first over the barn and the surrounding trees and then pressure-washing the air around them as it pounded the roof and the gravel and everything standing in its way. Even the cover of the little porch roof couldn't shelter them as the storm reached in from all directions, seeking them out. A branch from the oak nearest the house finally could stand it no more, and with an unnerving crack it tumbled to the ground.

"What in the world are you doing out there?" Bob shouted through the screen door behind them, but his voice was barely audible above the din. Now hail pinged and bounced about them; Charlotte had seen quite enough of the show.

"It came up so suddenly," she explained, turning back inside with the dog. Bob stepped back as Toby shook herself dry and Charlotte grabbed a towel that hung on the refrigerator handle.

"I have an idea," she told him from under the towel, just as another clap of thunder shook the house.

"What did you say?" Bob yelled over the din.

"I said, I have an idea about how we should handle this Troy Vanderveen fellow."

"Who?"

"Troy Vanderveen. The boy I told you about that Emily's been seeing."

"Oh, *that* Troy Vanderveen."

"That's what I said. I was thinking we can't just let him drive up and take Emily away, the way Kevin took Denise."

"Don't know if we have a choice in the matter."

"Well, we do. I told Emily she could invite him to her birthday dinner tonight," Charlotte informed Bob. "We need to make an effort to get to know him in a friendly way. So at least Emily won't be clinging to him because she thinks Grandma and Grandpa don't approve."

"Get to know him, huh?" Bob didn't look impressed, but he nodded his head as he padded back to his chair, the sports pages in hand. "A little reverse psychology—you think that'll make any difference?"

Charlotte couldn't answer with any certainty. All she knew was the storm had apparently spent its energy on their farm, and was passing on as quickly as it had arrived.

TRUE TO HER WORD, Emily made it home promptly at four thirty, dropped off by a giggling carful of girls with Ashley at the wheel. As Charlotte peeked out the kitchen window at them, she decided it could have been worse.

Emily burst through the back door, trailing pink-and-blue birthday streamers. She dumped a gift bag of goodies on the kitchen table.

"Did you have fun hanging with your friends?" asked Charlotte, but Emily was already headed up the stairs.

"It was great. Don't have time to talk. Gotta take a shower and get dressed before Troy gets here!"

"Oh, so he's coming?" Charlotte wondered out loud.

"She's taking a shower *again?*" Christopher wandered in from the living room, where he had been reading the newspaper comics on the floor after getting home from Dylan's. He spied a candy bar in his sister's gift bag on the kitchen table. "Hey, do you want this, Emily?" he yelled up the stairs.

He reached for the prize but Charlotte warned him off. Emily had already disappeared into the upstairs bathroom.

"Don't you dare," she told him.

"But she doesn't like this kind."

"Doesn't matter. You ask her nicely a little later, and she might share."

Christopher screwed up his face in a frown and then sniffed.

"I doubt it. Sounds like she has a hot date. And what's that smell?"

Charlotte didn't mention the meatless meatloaf.

"It's not a hot date," she told him, "just Troy Vanderveen coming over for dinner. And if you behave, you might get some birthday cake for dessert."

"Birthday cake!" That seemed to satisfy the candy thief as he pumped his fist. "Yes!"

"Grandma!" Emily shouted from upstairs. "I can't find any shampoo. Can you—?"

Charlotte scurried upstairs to help just as a knock at the back door told her Emily's "hot date" had arrived. Was he a few minutes early? Charlotte stepped back down just far enough to catch Bob's attention with a wave.

"That's him!" she said in a stage whisper while pointing in the direction of the back door. "Open the door!"

Bob grabbed a small pad of paper from the table next to his chair before standing and straightening. She waved again, and he nodded. What was he mumbling to himself? Get to know him better?

Charlotte didn't have time to wonder as she helped Emily find the shampoo she was missing and then the blouse that might have been dropped in the wash. What she saw when she came down ten minutes later made her wish she'd answered the door herself.

Actually she heard the uncomfortable exchange on her way down, and she stopped in her tracks.

"Then what are your job prospects?" Bob grilled Troy.

"Well, sir, I'm just a junior and I work part-time for now," Troy stammered.

"Are you planning to go to college? You know it's hard to make a living these days without a degree," Bob continued.

"Well, I sort of thought I'd take this summer to check around. You know, visit . . ."

Troy's voice trailed off into an awkward silence.

Charlotte couldn't stand it any longer and pretended to cough as she stomped down the stairs. Was this how Bob was getting to know Troy? The poor boy had a finger hooked into his collar and was obviously sweating when he looked up at Charlotte with a profound expression of gratitude. He jumped to his feet like a gentleman, which she hoped he was.

"Mrs. Stevenson!" He smiled and extended his hand, obviously relieved he didn't have to answer Bob's last question. "Nice to meet you."

Charlotte smiled back and did her best to set their guest at ease with small talk until Emily came tripping down the stairs a few minutes later. She wore the cute blue top Charlotte had helped her find, along with a nicer pair of jeans.

Bob frowned at the appreciative look Troy gave her just as Pete and Dana knocked at the door. The kitchen soon filled with the laughter of their guests and the warm smells of meatless meatloaf, steaming creamed corn, green beans, and rolls. And of course Christopher had discovered Emily's birthday cake on the counter.

"Don't touch!" Charlotte warned him before he nearly poked a finger into the vanilla frosting.

"You mean we're not having dessert first?" Pete asked, an arm around his wife and an eye on the food. Charlotte hoped Troy didn't try anything like that with Emily.

When the time came, Emily and Troy sat pretty close

together at the dinner table. A leaf in the middle made it large enough to seat all eight of them. She was almost relieved that Bill and Anna and the kids had had other plans and weren't able to join them today. Sam breezed in the back door and slipped into his empty chair just as Bob cleared his throat to say grace.

"Sorry I'm late," Sam mumbled.

"Glad you could make it," said Bob, his head still bowed. He recited a brief prayer as Emily slipped her hand under the table—presumably to hold Troy's.

"Amen," Pete said after his father finished. "Dig in."

So they did, passing meatloaf and creamed corn and a pitcher of milk around the table.

"We pass what's left to the left," Christopher told their guest, who had begun to pass the beans against the tide.

"Oh." Troy reversed course. "That makes sense."

"Troy only has an older sister," explained Emily. "He's not used to big family dinners."

"But this is fun," Troy told them, venturing a grin. Over on the other end of the table, Pete and his dad were all about the serious business of eating.

"Great meatloaf, Mom," Pete told her between mouthfuls.

Charlotte winked at Emily. With all the ketchup her son had squirted onto his portion, he obviously couldn't tell the difference between crumbled veggie burger with spices and breadcrumbs and real beef. Christopher could, but she warned him with her eyes not to say a word and for once he complied, washing down his carefully chewed mouthfuls with copious swigs of milk.

As they ate Charlotte meant to ask Dana how things

were going at school, but she didn't get a chance before talk turned to the house-building project and how ticked off Pete still was about the vandalism.

"They ever find who did it?" asked Bob. Pete shook his head and looked as if he wanted to spit.

"Not yet," replied Pete, helping himself to another roll. "But the deputy says he thinks he knows who it was. Says he's going to nail 'em. When he does, I'm going to give those clowns a piece of my mind too."

"I saw a truck over there that night," Christopher announced. Suddenly everyone stopped eating and looked at him.

"You never told us about that," said Pete, but Christopher just shrugged.

"I didn't know for sure 'cause it was just a dark truck and I couldn't see much."

As this conversation unfolded, Charlotte glanced at Troy, who seemed to be shrinking in his seat. If the young man had looked nervous earlier while Bob was grilling him, now he looked positively numb, perhaps pale, and he rubbed his forehead with the serious effort of a masseuse. As Pete went on about what he was going to do to the vandals, Troy shifted in his seat and glanced at the back door as if planning an escape.

"You don't like the meatloaf either, huh?" Christopher asked him from across the table. Leave it to Christopher to blurt out the obvious. "That's OK. I saw what Grandma put in it. You want to know?"

"Christopher!" Charlotte scolded him. "Mind your manners. And don't you ever give away my secret recipe, if you know what's good for you."

"I like it just fine." Troy sat up straight and swallowed hard, not convincing anyone. "It's really good, Mrs. Stevenson. Honest."

Everyone else at the table added their mandatory nods of agreement as Troy took another bite. His hand actually seemed to shake, proving one thing for certain: Something had obviously spooked the boy. But what?

Chapter
Twenty-One

After dinner that night the house seemed to clear as quickly as it had filled. Dana, who had hardly said a word all evening, apparently had to prepare for work, so she and Pete left once the dishes had been cleared. Bob had a project out in the barn, Sam was off to see his friends again, Christopher disappeared to check on Magic, and Emily and Troy said they were going out for a walk.

Charlotte was left standing alone in the kitchen, listening to the sudden quiet. And really, there was only one thing to do about it, in her estimation: finish cleaning the house.

Armed with what she thought was her best idea of the day —certainly easier than trying to make Troy Vanderveen's acquaintance—she assembled her housekeeping arsenal from the hallway closet and set to work with a vengeance. If nothing else, perhaps this would help get her mind off her worries about Sam's schoolwork and Pete's house and Emily's romance.

It gave her a certain small degree of satisfaction to demolish several cobwebs with her vacuum cleaner as she worked her way up the staircase, one step at a time.

Next came the second-floor hallway, and she kicked aside mounds of dirty clothes in each of the kids' rooms. The wastebaskets appeared as if they hadn't been emptied this calendar year.

The good news was that the contents of their trash gave Charlotte clues as to the kids' recent behavior. Christopher's trash, for example, included several candy wrappers. They would need to talk about that. In Sam's room she stooped to pick up crumpled papers around his wicker basket and couldn't help noticing a letterhead that read "Office of Admissions and Records, Central Community College, Grand Island, Nebraska."

What was this? Feeling like a sleuth—or a snoop—she straightened the crumpled letter:

"Dear Mr. Slater: Thank you for your interest in attending CCC in the fall and for submitting your application. We're pleased to inform you that you have been provisionally accepted to our fall semester program, pending completion of your high school graduation requirements. As an open-door campus, CCC welcomes students from across central Nebraska, and does not discriminate on the basis of . . ."

Sam had been accepted at Central Community College? Charlotte looked nervously over her shoulder, imagining what would happen if Sam showed up just now and caught her going through his trash—and reading his mail, no less!

What had kept Sam from mentioning that he had been accepted to a college in the fall: Wasn't this excellent news? News to celebrate?

She understood Central Community College admitted

nearly any high school graduate who applied, which was why it was called an open-door school. At the same time, Charlotte had always heard good things about its programs. And Grand Island was the perfect location, only about forty miles north. It wasn't a bad drive, except on the worst days of winter, when roads iced up. Sam could commute and save on living expenses.

In fact, the more she thought about it, the more perfect it seemed. He could take the computer classes that interested him, and she and Bob and the kids wouldn't exactly have to say good-bye just yet. She might even help him with his laundry, and she and Bob could still have some influence on their grandson's life.

What's more, with Sam close to home he could still be a daily part of his younger siblings' lives, if he wanted to. It wouldn't be the same as if he left home to attend a school across the state—or the country. He could still be based here at the farm.

"This is perfect!" she said out loud, just as the back door slammed.

"I'm home!" Sam announced. His timing seemed impeccable, and his announcement made her scurry about in a bit of a panic, pushing her supplies and her vacuum out the door and stuffing the crumpled letter into her pocket.

"Anybody home?" he called up the stairs. Bob must have fallen asleep in front of the TV. No one else answered.

"I'm up here!" she called back, and a moment later Sam met her at the door to his room. The young man could certainly fly up those stairs when he wanted to. And now he studied his grandmother with the vacuum, the full garbage bag, and the cleaning supplies.

"What's up?" he asked her. "I didn't know my room needed cleaning."

"Well, it was either this," she replied, "or have the fire department come in with a high-pressure hose to clear it out."

Somehow he didn't find that extremely funny. They exchanged a couple more stiff pleasantries, she finding out that none of his friends were home after all, and he learning what kind of leftovers might remain in the refrigerator. But as she traded places with him and squeezed out with all her cleaning equipment, she felt for the crumpled letter in her pocket and summoned enough nerve to say what she really needed to say—before he had a chance to close his door and turn up his stereo.

"Uh, Sam." She scooted the vacuum aside with her foot. "There's actually something I need to ask you."

He lifted his eyebrows in a *Well?*

"I don't mean to pry, but when I was emptying your trash can I noticed a letter from Central Community College."

"Oh, that." His face fell, and he took on a trapped expression. She didn't know if he would say anything else.

"Yes, that. We knew you had applied, but you never said anything about being accepted." She paused when he didn't answer. "In any case, I think it could be a wonderful place for you. They have computer classes there, don't they?"

"I guess so." Sam shrugged. "Didn't get a chance to read the catalog much."

"All right, but why would you crumple the letter?" She pulled it from her pocket and straightened it out a little more before extending it to him.

"Doesn't matter," he told her, keeping his arms folded in

front of him in a sort of defiant pose. "I'm not going there anyway."

"I don't understand. Here's a place with the classes you want, close to home, and you're already accepted. Why would you not at least consider it?"

He didn't answer right away, just shrugged and turned aside. But he wasn't going to get away with an I-don't-know answer. Charlotte was determined now to get to the bottom of this.

"Your other friends are going to college, aren't they?" she asked. "Most of them, I mean."

"Some of them. But definitely not to CCC."

"You say that as if it's a terrible place. You haven't even seen the campus."

"Paul has. He says . . ."

His voice trailed off, and Charlotte was beginning to get a clue now.

"What did Paul say? Why doesn't he like the school?"

"He says that only losers go to CCC." Sam sighed, as if he really didn't want to be having this conversation. "But it's not just him. Everybody says the same thing."

"Everybody? Somehow I doubt it. Here—I want you to keep this." She tapped his shoulder with the letter. "Let's not burn our bridges yet. I honestly think you could do well at CCC, and I don't think Paul should be bad-mouthing a place he obviously knows nothing about."

Sam finally and reluctantly accepted the letter from her, but he didn't promise not to toss it right back into the wastebasket as soon as she left the room.

What else could she do?

"Oh, and one other thing I've been meaning to ask you." She stood her ground. "The letter said your acceptance was conditional on your getting your diploma. How's that senior project coming along that you still need to do?"

"It's under control, Grandma." He reached for his door handle now, even before she'd made it all the way out. "Just trust me on this, OK? I mean, I appreciate what you're saying, but really. It's OK."

"Is it? Wait a minute, Sam." Charlotte didn't want to get into a tug-of-war with Sam's bedroom door, but neither did she want the conversation to end this way. Goodness gracious! Hadn't she just been in the same position with Emily—on the outside of a bedroom door? She held on to her side of the doorknob as tightly as she could while doing her best to keep her voice steady and put in a last word.

"I'd like to trust you to do the right thing, Sam. But I'm worried that you're not taking this project seriously despite what you tell me—and your teachers."

"But I am—"

"No, listen. Please." Charlotte had no idea why this had to be so hard. Why did everything with these kids have to be so hard lately? Sam just stared at her as she braced herself outside his door, almost nose to nose.

"This project isn't just some annoying assignment you can blow off," she said, struggling to hold her annoyance in check. "We're talking about the rest of your life, dear, and it starts with graduation. Your Uncle Pete had the same attitude, and I believe he's regretted not finishing high school. That isn't so difficult to see, is it? And the same goes for this letter from the college. It's an opportunity you're being given. An open door. Please, *please* don't let it just close in your face."

She finally loosened her grip on the door. As she did, Sam paused for just a moment.

"Thanks, Grandma," he told her, but without any indication that he really meant what he said. "I promise you I'll take care of it."

CHRISTOPHER COULD SEE everything from where he hid in the dark barn, and he felt like a spy as he watched his sister and Troy walking back to where Troy's truck was parked by the house.

Hand in hand. Eeew.

Was it really the same truck he'd seen the other night? Christopher squinted again and tried to recall, but the memory now seemed a little fuzzy. Maybe it was, and maybe it wasn't. All he knew for sure was that Emily seemed to really like Troy, and Troy had tried to help him with Magic. Maybe that counted for something.

Christopher's mind spun as Troy slipped into his truck and started the engine with a familiar-sounding roar.

Troy wouldn't have done anything bad to Uncle Pete's house, he thought. *He wouldn't spray-paint that bunch of windows.*

Would he?

Chapter
Twenty-Two

Sam couldn't wait for school to let out. But then there was this weird little part of him that kind of wished the bell wouldn't ring after all. He wasn't used to that kind of feeling. But in a sort of fantasy way, he figured if it didn't ring then maybe he could just hide in class the rest of that day and not have to explain to anybody that he still didn't have a clue what he should do for his stupid senior project.

If he could hide, then he wouldn't have to explain to anybody that he was stuck on the whole thing, that he wasn't going to get it done, and that he probably wouldn't be able to graduate.

"Hey, wait up, you!" Arielle caught up with him in the parking lot, and he was relieved and not, all at the same time. "You weren't going to leave without me, were you?"

Her smile melted him like butter in the microwave, the way it always did. He was really enjoying spending time with her again and didn't want to mess things up.

"Uh, no." He tried to sound normal. "Just have to pick up Christopher, you know."

Arielle gave him a funny look.

"I thought you said your grandma was taking him and Emily to the dentist this afternoon."

He had to think about that for a moment. Had he said that?

"Oh, yeah. Forgot." He finally remembered as he tossed his books into the storage area behind the ripped-up front seats of his little car. Arielle caught him by the hand before he could climb inside the almost-classic 240-Z.

"Sam!" She caught his eye, and her voice kind of shook. "I know all about your senior project."

He broke free and climbed in behind the wheel, wondering where he could hide. If Arielle knew, she would be freaking out for sure. Maybe she didn't know quite everything.

"You do?" He asked as she climbed in beside him.

"You think it's a secret." She closed the door. "But I know you've put it off. I heard."

He sighed and stared straight ahead, gripping the steering wheel but not starting the car. She shocked him by reaching over and taking his hand.

"Sam! You're acting like a little kid. If you didn't know what to do, why didn't you ask for help?"

He shrugged. "It might be too late anyway."

"No, it's not."

The weird thing was, her voice sounded just as soft as ever. Like she knew what a loser he was and still wasn't upset. This was a big turnaround from a few months ago when she broke up with him. He couldn't really believe she would be so understanding about this. Finally he peeked over at her as she went on.

"I might have a great idea for you—I mean, only if you want it. I don't want to tell you what to do."

"Hey, at this point I'll do anything that'll get me out of this mess."

"All right." She nodded and pointed down the street. "Then drive."

"Huh?" He didn't understand. That wouldn't be the way home for either of them.

"Don't worry; just drive. That way. We're going to the church. You'll see."

"Uh, OK. But you're going to explain what this is all about, right?"

"You'll find out."

By this time she looked as if she were enjoying this little treasure hunt, or whatever it was. She stifled a grin as he put the car in gear and they headed down Lincoln Street toward Bedford Community Church. A few minutes later, she was leading him by the hand through the church's side door and into the little office area. The church secretary was out, and Jason Vink sat hunched over his computer keyboard, hunting and pecking with the utmost concentration. Because of his size he had to scrunch himself closer, as if the computer were too small for someone like him to use. Finally Arielle cleared her throat and he jolted upright.

"Whoa!" He looked at them with wide-eyed surprise before sliding into an easy smile and leaning back in his chair. "Didn't hear you come in. What's up?"

He wore a gray Nebraska Christian College T-shirt and a pair of raggedy jeans.

Arielle didn't waste any time getting straight to the point. "We need a good senior service project. Something that we can do this month, I mean. Like, right away."

Sam noticed she said *we* rather than *he*, and he wasn't

quite sure why she included herself in this deal. But it did sound nicer, so he didn't interrupt as she continued.

"I was thinking . . . you're involved with that group that builds houses for low-income families, aren't you?"

"You wanna know about Shelter for Nebraska, huh?" His smile broadened when he understood why they'd come. But the way Arielle talked about it, Sam thought maybe he was supposed to know what this group was all about. He kept his mouth shut and just nodded when Jason looked at him. He supposed he would find out soon enough.

"I haven't told the youth group yet," he explained, "because SFN just started working in our part of the state, and I just got on their board. But since you asked . . ."

He showed them some brochures from the group, which apparently was all about building homes for poor people. That sounded pretty decent to Sam. As far as he could tell, church people, youth groups and other community members volunteered their time to do the building. Jason got more worked up the more he talked about it; he seemed to be smiling all over because they were showing interest.

"Would you guys like to join a project? I've got one in Grand Island that'll probably start next month—mostly doing framing—and then one in Harding that's already half done. It just needs finish work, which takes longer than you expect sometimes, especially if you can't get enough volunteers."

Arielle looked at Sam with a smile and asked him, "What do you think?"

"I think it sounds cool," replied Sam, "except I don't

know anything about building houses."

"You don't need to," replied Jason. "All you do is show up for a weekend or two or three. Or as much as you can. The project foreman will tell you exactly what you need to do, and all the supplies and equipment are provided. You just show up. Piece of cake."

Sam looked at the brochures a little more. Not that he could afford to be picky at this late date, but this kind of project really didn't look too bad at all—especially if it was a *we* project and not just a *me* project. Arielle looked almost as smiley about it as Jason did.

"I think it sounds great," she said. "And I know Mr. Santos would think it's a perfect senior service project."

"Next weekend in Harding then?" Jason jotted their names on a pad of paper. "I was actually hoping for a few more volunteers for this one. This will help. We need painters and finish carpenters and cleanup people and gofers—just about everything. But like I said, don't worry for a minute, 'cause you definitely don't need to be an expert. They'll tell you just what you need to do."

So that was it? Arielle slipped her hand into Sam's as they walked back to his car, and that was worth the price of admission, right there. With her along he figured he might be able to handle this assignment, after all.

"See?" she told him. "That wasn't so hard, was it?"

"Well . . ."

Actually no, it wasn't. And though he wouldn't admit it even to Arielle, he wondered why it had taken him so long to figure out something as simple as this.

"PERFECT!" The next evening Uncle Pete acted almost as excited about the whole Shelter for Nebraska thing as Jason and Arielle had been just the day before. "Why didn't you think of this before it got to be a crisis?"

"Pete!" Grandma scolded him as she boiled some potato stuff on the stove while Christopher set the table with the knives upside-down and the spoons on the wrong side. "He doesn't need to hear your criticism too. I think he's already heard enough of that from me. The main thing is, he has a project now."

"It's all right," Sam told them, leaning against the wall. Really, he didn't mind telling them this time. For once he had something to say that wouldn't start an argument. "It actually wasn't my idea though. Arielle heard about it from Jason, and he only just got hooked up with the SFN thing last month; he's on their board of directors, or something like that. He thinks maybe the whole youth group might help with another project later this year."

"The SFN thing?" asked Christopher.

"Shelter for Nebraska." Sam tried to sound as if he knew what he was talking about. "And you should have heard Mr. Santos; he was all over it when I told him today at school. Like it was the greatest idea I ever came up with."

"Or he was just relieved you came up with *something*," said Uncle Pete.

"Peter Stevenson, you stop teasing!" Charlotte told him.

"He's a big boy, Mom; he can take it," he said, fending her off with a smile.

"Your wife is probably wondering where you are," she said. "It's dinnertime, you know."

But he only shook his head.

"I don't think so," he said, lowering his voice. "She's got another school-board meeting tonight."

Sam didn't miss the look between Grandma and Grandpa, like some kind of secret signal. Bottom line, they didn't look too happy. Still, Uncle Pete pointed back at Sam as he made his exit.

"I'll let you borrow a tool belt, kid," he said. "Any tools you need. You just let me know." Apparently he hadn't heard the part about how Sam was probably only going to be painting. Sam gave his uncle a thumbs-up and thanked him.

For a change, Sam was actually a little bit proud of himself. Now maybe he would graduate from high school after all.

Chapter Twenty-Three

I should call you Bob the Ripper," Charlotte told her husband as she loaded the washer Wednesday afternoon. Honestly, she couldn't believe the way he treated his jeans.

Bob leaned against the kitchen counter as he downed a cold glass of milk for his midday snack. "Sorry. We were working on some barbed wire. Guess the knee kind of caught."

"Kind of? I'm tossing these jeans in the rag bag."

"Hey! Those are some of my favorite jeans."

"Were." She adjusted the load and restarted her old machine, wondering how many jeans it had washed in the past twenty years.

"And by the way, do you know what happened with Pete and his boundary issue?"

"His business." Bob shook his head. "I barely see him anymore unless I go over there to check on how his house is coming."

"I take that to mean he hasn't figured it out yet."

"Yeah, well, he doesn't seem too worried; he's pushing ahead with construction."

"But what if it turns out he's wrong? What if he's really building on the neighbor's property?"

"Now you're sounding like Walt Freeman. You should have heard him down at AA this morning, spouting off like he's been watching too many lawyer shows on TV."

"Walt's still upset?"

"You could say that. I'd be taking him more seriously if I were Pete."

Charlotte added a stray shirt to the washer load and shook her head.

"Well, I don't like the whole thing, and I don't know why Pete doesn't just take care of it. It's still officially our property, you know. I think we ought to have something to say about the matter, don't you?"

Bob finished his milk and wiped his milk mustache with the back of his hand before setting the glass in the sink and heading for the back door.

"Like I said, I'm not going to poke my nose in his business. I'll let you know if I hear anything."

So that was it, as far as Bob was concerned. He left again to return to his fieldwork, leaving Charlotte with her hands on her hips.

Is there really nothing we can do? she wondered.

While Charlotte was still pondering the problem, Christopher ambled into the kitchen and parked himself next to the washing machine, his nose buried in the S volume of the old *Encyclopaedia Britannica*.

"Did you come down to help me fold clothes?" asked Charlotte. Christopher answered with a shake of his head.

"Not my business. It's Emily's job."

"You men are all alike."

"Huh?" Christopher, of course, didn't get it.

"Never mind. Speaking of Emily, is she off with Ashley again? She didn't come home with you from school, did she?"

Christopher shook his head once more, never taking his eyes off the book.

"Troy," he told her, frowning. Enough said.

She sighed. "I should have known. I suppose she'll have to tend to her chores when she gets back for dinner, won't she?"

Either Christopher didn't hear her, or he'd found something highly interesting inside the pages of his dog-eared encyclopedia. Pete, Bill, and Denise had used that dusty old set of books for their homework years ago. Did anyone even still read encyclopedias anymore? Seems like everything that used to be printed was now on the Internet or on an I-something. Without warning Christopher jabbed at the page and looked up at her with wild eyes.

"Maybe Magic has white-muscle disease," he announced, bending a little more closely to read. "Says here with white-muscle disease the lamb will have trouble walking, and it's due to a lack of . . ."

He paused to pronounce the next word slowly and carefully.

". . . selenium or vitamin E. What's selenium?"

"Just a mineral that animals need," she answered. "But what happened to the idea that your lamb ate poison hemlock?"

"He did. But I still think he's acting kinda funny."

"Are you sure? Because the last I heard, your Uncle Pete

thought he looked fine."

"Maybe." He returned to the book, his brow still wrinkled. "But look what it says here: 'Scrapie, or wasting disease. Affected sheep rub their head or rump against fences or buildings and then develop tremors or con ... con-vul-sions, leading to death.' That sounds yucky."

"Has he been acting that way?"

"He does act itchy sometimes."

"All right. But you know your lamb doesn't have scrapie, dear."

"Then there's the lack of colo—"

"Colostrum."

"Right. Says here 75 percent of sheep that don't get it, die. I don't want Magic to die!"

"Christopher. You don't need to worry so much. God has his hand on that sheep, don't you think? And we all have to die sooner or later. In this case, I'd bet it's going to be a lot later. But—"

"But we still have to find out what's making him sick!"

"Wait a minute. Don't you think his tummy was just upset from eating the wrong things? You got rid of those noxious weeds around his pen after you found out."

"After Troy told me."

"Yes, so—"

"Maybe it's pneumonia. It could be that, don't you think?"

"Christopher, you're not listening. You don't need to worry like this. In fact, I don't believe your lamb has any of those things. He looks fine to me too."

"But Grandma, how do you know? He doesn't eat as

much as all the other lambs in the 4-H club. He's the small-est, compared to all the rest. We need to find out what's wrong, and then we need to fix it!"

Charlotte looked down at her young grandson, trying to decipher the worry on his face. Once more he leafed through the "sheep diseases" section of the encyclopedia, desperately searching for answers. Finally she reached down, gently closed the book, and rested her hands on his shoulders.

"Is there anything else bothering you, dear?"

He shook his head with vigor and gripped the book as if she might grab it from his hands. Naturally he would deny anything was wrong. He was a boy, after all, and he took after his grandfather that way. Perhaps he didn't actually know what was wrong, but Charlotte felt nearly certain there was *something else.*

"How about you forget about Magic for a little while," she finally told him. "Maybe you could go find out what your brother is up to?"

"He's not here, Grandma. He's gone with his friends. He's always gone with his friends."

"Oh, well. You know he's been spending a lot of time with them lately before they all go their separate ways."

"Yeah, but when he goes off to college, he's . . . not going to come back!"

Christopher turned his head to the side and rubbed his forehead, obviously shielding his eyes. But Charlotte caught the look of pain and the quivering lip.

"Oh, Christopher! Is that what it is? You're worried about Sam leaving?" She dropped the towel in her hands and stooped down to give him a hug. To her surprise, he latched on and would not let go while she patted him on the back and tried to think of words to encourage a little brother with a breaking heart.

"A kid at school told me his big brother went off to college," he told her, "and then he got married, and then he moved to Dallas, Texas. After that he never came home, not even for Christmas."

"Well, you're probably going off to college too in a few years. You'll see that it's not so bad. It's just part of life for a lot of kids."

"Not me. I'm going to stay here with Magic."

"What about being a weatherman, the way you've said before? You have to go to college if you want to be a weatherman. You couldn't stay here."

"Hmm. Forgot about that." He seemed to weigh that option again for a minute. "Still, I don't want Sam to move to Dallas, Texas."

"To tell you the truth, I don't either. But I don't think that's what Sam has in mind."

"You don't know for sure though, do you? Just like you don't know about Magic for sure."

"Maybe not." She had an idea. "Tell you what. If I let you in on a little secret, will you promise not to tell?"

He sniffled on the back of his hand and pulled back for a better view, as if to weigh whether her secret might be important enough for a deal.

"What kind of secret?" he finally asked.

"All right, here's the thing." By this time Charlotte's knees and back were beginning to give out from all the stooping. She moved over to a kitchen chair and pulled up another chair for Christopher to join her. "I'm sure your brother's going to choose what's best, and that may even mean going away for a little while. I can't promise you anything." Now she lowered her voice. "But I happen to know that he's already been accepted at a college in Grand Island. All he has to do is tell them yes or no."

"Grand Island?" Christopher's face brightened a little. "That's not too far, is it? Dylan has an aunt who lives in Grand Island, and she comes for dinner all the time."

"Exactly!" She leaned even closer, nose to nose. "But you have to remember, your brother hasn't actually decided yet, and I don't think he's told anybody else. So you can't just go up to him and say you know. See what I mean?"

He nodded his head like a true conspirator, holding a finger to his sealed lips. Good.

"And if he decides not to go there," she told him, "that's completely up to him, and it's OK."

He nodded gravely as she went on.

"But here's what you can do. If the subject comes up, and I think it probably will, you can say that you really like the idea of him going to college in Grand Island instead of someplace else."

"Because that way, he could still be home. Sometimes."

"You got it." She smiled at him as she pretended to spit in her right palm before extending it for him to shake. "Do we have a secret deal?"

Unfortunately, Christopher's spit wasn't pretend. But she shook his hand anyway. It would be a small price to pay for cheering up a grandson and enlisting him in her cause. She wiped her hand on a dish towel as she stepped over to the freezer.

"You know what this calls for?" she asked. "This calls for some rocky-road ice cream and a couple of chocolate chip cookies."

"Grandma!" He stepped up beside her. "What about spoiling your appetite before dinner?"

"Never mind that," she replied. "It's just for today: dessert first."

"Hmm." He gladly found an ice-cream scoop in the utensil drawer and a couple of bowls in the cupboard. "I could get used to this."

Charlotte could too if she wasn't careful. In any case, it was a whole lot better than wrestling with Bob's ripped jeans.

Chapter Twenty-Four

The next day after school Emily shuffled around Sam's little car out in the parking lot, trying her best not to brush against it and wondering where to put her books. He really needed to wash the disgusting old thing. Of course, with all the different colors of paint and rust, he also really needed to paint it. She thought a nice bright blue might be cheery, or maybe an aqua, but she knew Sam would never go along with that kind of color choice.

Besides, what was she thinking? He didn't have the money for a new paint job. Forget it. She looked around the parking lot again, waving at a couple of girls from youth group as they were leaving with the rest of the after-school crowd. She didn't know them very well, but they slowed down in their little pickup truck, and one of them asked if she needed a ride.

"Thanks," she replied, trying her best to smile and remain polite, "but I'm waiting for my long-lost brother."

"Then you'll be waiting a long time," replied the driver, Brittany. Or was it Megan? "I saw him snuggling with Arielle in the library a few minutes ago."

"You did?" Not that she was surprised. Emily finally decided to leave her books on the hood and hurried back into the school to the nearly empty library. Sure enough, Sam and Arielle had huddled up pretty close together in front of one of three computer workstations, apparently lost to the world and actually much closer than they needed to be. She paused for a moment, frowning, before clearing her throat.

"Hey," she said, making no effort to disguise the impatience in her voice, "are we going home or what? Christopher's going to be wondering what's going on. I mean, we could have taken the bus . . ."

Sam jerked his head around as if she'd startled him, and Emily thought she noticed Arielle's cheeks redden.

"Uh, sorry." Sam straightened up. "Were you waiting? We were just working on the write-up for my service project. Lost track of time, I guess."

"Yeah, I could tell."

Emily hoped Arielle would get the hint.

"I'd better go," said Arielle, checking her watch. "You think we can finish—"

"Sure. Tomorrow. Whenever." Sam gathered up his stuff and his backpack as he quit the computer program. "Meet you at the car in five minutes, Emily."

"I'll be waiting," she answered and then turned on her heel and headed back through the hallways to the parking lot. Her brother could sure act goofy and immature sometimes with this girlfriend of his. No way anyone would catch her acting that way with Troy. She pushed through the school's front doors and headed for the car once again.

Speaking of Troy, wasn't that him at the far end of the parking lot, near the football-field bleachers? She might have waved to him, but he wasn't looking her way. Instead he seemed locked into a pretty intense conversation with two other guys.

Even at a distance she recognized the other two as trouble —kids who slouched in the back rows of class, if they bothered to show up at all, and who were more than likely into the drug scene. They might have been fifty yards away, but there was no mistaking the heat of the back-and-forth as Troy waved his arms and raised his voice at them.

But as much as he seemed to yell at them, they threw strong talk right back at him. Emily couldn't quite make out the words, but she was pretty sure they were not polite or repeatable. And judging by the way they leaned into the confrontation from all sides, she was almost surprised it hadn't yet come to blows. One of the kids tried to walk away at one point, but Troy grabbed him by the collar and spun him around. Emily winced, expecting the worst.

Luckily Troy released his grip. He turned away and stomped off, leaving them cursing and gesturing. When he saw her standing in front of the flagpole, his face turned from night to day, just like that.

"There you are!" he said, trotting up to her as if nothing had happened. She couldn't avoid the unmistakable smell of cigarette smoke on his clothes, even standing outside like this. "I was looking for you."

She took an involuntary step back, still shocked at what she had seen.

"What was that all about?"

"Oh, that?" The smile never left his face as he waved dismissively to the side. "That was nothing. Just a friendly conversation."

"Friendly? You mean, like they're your friends?"

He chewed on that for just a second before answering.

"I know 'em. They get excited a little too easily about things that don't matter. Trust me. It's nothing. I'm . . . not like they are."

Done. End of story. Troy obviously didn't want to talk about the matter any further. But Emily still couldn't shake her uneasy feeling as he took her hand and told her he'd give her a ride home.

"Well, I guess it would be OK." She looked over her shoulder at the front doors of the school just in time to see Sam emerge. He saw her and stopped in his tracks as she waved at him. She was sure he would understand.

But he didn't wave back.

OVER IN HARDING, Pete parked his old pickup, Lazarus, in front of the little frame building that housed the county courthouse and the office of the County Records and Planning Department. Even with his key turned to the off position, the engine rattled on for a few more seconds until it finally wheezed to a stop. He gave it an A for effort. His old truck never wanted to quit.

As he sat in the truck, Pete gathered his papers and his thoughts, making sure he had everything. He almost wheezed himself—some lousy cold coming on. Just now, he wasn't feeling as sure of himself as he had before. Maybe that's why he'd put off this second visit so long. He hoped it would only take a minute now to double-check the land records.

Heck, what did he have to worry about? He had all the documents he needed to show them that he was building in the right place—the surveys, the bill of sale, all that. They would probably have copies of the same stuff on file. This was just a formality. Pete was sure he had nothing to worry about.

Pretty sure.

He shoved open the truck's door and entered the office with a confident stride. He didn't have an appointment, but he figured Tim Olson, the county planner, would have a free moment.

A couple of minutes later he was sitting in Tim's cluttered little office surrounded by detailed county property maps tacked up on every wall. Piles of charts and papers weighed down the older man's desk—assuming there was a desk somewhere under that sea of paper. It seemed almost alive and breathing. A pipe smoldered somewhere underneath. Wasn't there a law against smoking in public buildings? Tim, a bit overweight and well into his sixties, tipped his half-frame reading glasses back over his head, scratched his bald dome, and squinted at the property sketch Pete had handed him.

"Hmm. I thought so." He reached to his right under a particularly tall stack of manila folders, fishing out a large, round magnifying glass. Pete wondered how the man could have known it was there under all that stuff. He was troubled by the look on Tim's face.

"Something wrong?" asked Pete.

The planner didn't answer right away, just took one of Pete's documents in his hand and padded over to a row of file cabinets out in the hall. Pete followed him, not sure if he should press for more details just yet.

"You know where we sited the house," Pete explained, "just this side of the border between our property and Walt Freeman's, way off in the corner. It's a little rise where nobody's been planting for a long time. But there's a great view."

"I know." Tim shuffled through a few more files, pulling out paper after paper. The guy really seemed to have a way with paper. "That's why I had you come back in after your first visit. I've been doing some more research, and . . ."

"And?" Pete didn't like the sound of it.

"And you won't like what I found out."

"But . . ." Pete's throat went dry. "You've seen the paper that shows my grandfather bought that little piece of land on the border between the Freeman place and ours. See?"

"Bob should have known better," Tim mumbled.

"No, you don't understand. Bob, I mean my dad, doesn't have anything to do with this."

"You mean, he doesn't know?"

"He knows what Walt's saying, but he's busy with spring planting and stuff, and I've been handling the farm's legal paperwork for the last little while. I'm the one who found this old bill of sale. I thought it was clear that we owned that little strip of property where we're putting up the house."

"It might have looked clear to you." Tim slammed his

old file cabinet shut, sending up a cloud of dust. "Problem is, I've found out it's not legal."

"What do you mean, it's not legal? See those signatures? Right there. Victor Freeman—that's Walt's dad—and there, my grandpa. They had cool signatures back in the day, huh?"

"Looks nice; don't mean a thing." Tim shook his head and held up the yellowed and faded but still official-looking paper. "Far as I can tell, the deed was never recorded. So the land you think you own, you don't really own at all. Not legally, anyway."

"What?" Pete tried not to panic. "That's impossible."

"Impossible? Nope. Improbable? Yeah. Not to mention rare. I honestly don't know how this snafu could have been missed for so long. But it's not impossible. In fact, it's happened before, especially off in the back corners where nobody pays too much attention to a scrap of paper describing such a deal."

"But it's not—" Pete tried again as Tim shook his head.

"Far as I'm concerned, if it's not recorded, it's not legal. Wish you'd double-checked with me before this."

"But—"

"Look, we can do a more thorough check, jump through all the legal hoops. But it's gonna take some time; I'll tell you that. Meanwhile, best I can tell, your neighbor still legally owns that strip of property you're building on."

"No, no, wait. Isn't there something else you can check?"

"You asked for a quick answer; that's the quick answer."

Pete rubbed his forehead, feeling a headache coming on. He couldn't believe this was happening.

"What about all the work we've already done?"

Tim shrugged. "Looks to me like you've got two options. One, you can tear down what's there—and for your sake, I hope it's not much."

Pete's head swam when he thought of all the time and money they'd already put into the house—just to tear it all down? What would he tell Dana?

"The other option," Tim continued, "and this would most likely be much less painful from your perspective, would be to actually purchase that piece of land from Walt. That's assuming he's willing to sell. It's up to him. He's holding all the cards at this point. Here you go."

He extended the now-worthless old bill of sale back to Pete just as the phone rang on his desk.

"Gotta go, Pete. Sorry for the bad news, but you let me know if there's any way I can help, okay? Meanwhile, don't do any more building on that site until you check with me. Officially I should put a stop-work order on it, but I'm going to let you try to figure it out first."

He stepped back into the office and reached for the ringing telephone, leaving Pete standing next to the file cabinets and the gurgling water cooler, wondering how he'd gotten himself into such a mess. How could he not have known? Why hadn't someone told him before this? Surely there was some mistake.

The worst thing was, he now had a pretty good idea whose mistake it was—his own.

Chapter Twenty-Five

A little after five the next morning, Pete thought for sure he would beat his dad to the barn as he turned down the familiar driveway to his parents' place. Sure enough, the house looked dark and quiet under a pewter sky that allowed only the faintest hint of dawn to the east.

He'd arrived well before breakfast, but he was not really sure why an early arrival seemed so important today. He stifled a cough and tried to unstiffen his aching neck as Lazarus sighed to a stop in his usual place by the big barn doors. He rotated his shoulders. It seemed as if his whole upper body, head included, was setting up in concrete. What was this all about? He had gotten over strep throat just before the wedding, and he never got sick.

He was surprised to see weak shafts of a pale yellow glow oozing from inside the barn. Maybe his dad had forgotten to turn off the light the night before. It wouldn't be the first time. He unloaded himself from the truck, stretching this way and that to try and work out the kinks. Nothing seemed to help. At least he could work by himself for an hour or two; he wouldn't have to talk to anybody or explain his embarrassing bad news about the house to anyone.

But when Pete pulled the double doors aside he found his dad inside, on his knees, messing with a plow attachment. He didn't even look up as Pete stepped in. Typical Dad.

"Afternoon, Pete."

"Afternoon? Dad, what are you doing up so early?"

"Hmm." Dad looked at his watch. "Didn't realize."

Oh yes he did.

"You're the one who's retired, Dad. You don't need to be here so early in the morning. You've been working too hard."

"Well . . ." Pete's dad strained and grunted at a wrench. "I figured if I didn't get here, you probably wouldn't either. Thought you'd get to the building site first, the way you've been doing, and mosey on in around lunchtime. Or have you been there already?"

"No. I haven't been there just yet."

Pete really didn't want to get into all the details, and he really didn't want to explain why work on the house had abruptly stopped. But he supposed his dad had a right to know. Might as well get it over with.

"Tim Olson at the planning department thinks we're probably building on the Freemans' land."

If Pete's dad was surprised, he sure did a good job hiding it. But he did pause from his work to wipe his brow. Even at this time of the morning a guy could work up a sweat.

"Thought you had that all figured out," he said.

"I do. I mean, I did. Or I sure thought I did."

"Sounds like you didn't."

"Well, he says the deal between Walt's dad and Grandpa was never recorded, so it's no good. Even though we had the original bill of sale to prove it. So now Tim says we've got to buy that piece of borderland all over again—assuming Walt even wants to sell."

"Hmm. And if he doesn't?"

"Then we're supposed to tear it all down and start over."

"You prepared to do that?"

"What do you think?"

Sure, he could tear it all down. Theoretically. Maybe he would just have to put a match to all their hard work. But rebuilding? No way. Not for a long time, if ever.

His dad pointed in the direction of a toolbox near the front entry.

"Grab the socket set out of that for me, would you?"

Pete moved for the toolbox, wondering about his dad's words. "Dad, did you hear what I just said?"

"I heard you. I need a half-inch extension. Should be on the top tray."

Gritting his teeth in frustration, Pete retrieved the half-inch extension and tossed it to his dad, who plucked it out of the air with one hand and returned to his work. Pete could only stand there and shake his head.

"You sure you don't know anything else about that deal between your dad and Walt's?" asked Pete. "Any idea why it wasn't recorded?"

His dad grunted as he tightened another bolt. "No idea. Funny little piece of land where you're building. Never paid much attention to it since it wasn't plantable. Just kind of always assumed it was ours, though—I guess the same way you did."

Pete's dad continued to fuss with the attachment, not making much progress. Outside, a mourning dove got an early start, breaking the silence with its haunting call. Finally Pete's dad stopped fiddling with the plow, but he still didn't look at his son.

"Look, I'm sorry the deal's going south on you. Maybe I could . . . I don't know. You want me to talk to Freeman for you?"

"No." Pete turned aside to cough, and this time a wave of nausea nearly doubled him over. He was really starting to feel unwell. "I'll take care of that myself when I get a chance. Right now I just need to get outside and get some real work done for a change."

His dad finally looked at him, this time with a furrowed brow.

"You OK?"

"Just a little something I picked up. Feels like some kind of bug. Like my whole head is aching. Maybe you don't want to get too close. I'll get over it."

Or so he hoped. But as the day wore on the bug Pete had caught only grew worse. It seemed to spread throughout his body, spinning his stomach inside-out and locking his head in a vise-grip of pain. He managed to get through the lunch hour by gluing himself to the tractor seat and toughing his way through row after row of plowing. He didn't dare look back at his work for fear of seeing how crooked he'd made his furrows, and for fear of falling off into the newly turned dirt.

By early afternoon, he had to stop. When he tumbled off the tractor by the far side of the barn, his mother caught sight of him and came over to investigate.

Great, he thought. *She's the last one I want to see me like this.*

He even did his best to straighten up and look casual, as in *No big deal, Mom.* But he knew from experience there was no avoiding this mother's eagle eye.

"What's wrong with you?" she asked, coming up to him and wiping her hands on a flour-covered apron. Normally that would have been his cue to find out what she was baking. Cookies, maybe, or a pie? This time he couldn't stop his hands from shaking, and she didn't wait for an answer. She stepped up closer and felt his forehead.

"Just a little—" he began, but she didn't let him finish.

"You're burning up, Pete. How long have you been this way?"

"Started feeling a little queasy this morning," he admitted. "Achy. You know."

No use trying to act like Mr. Tough Guy around Mom. She wouldn't buy it for a second. Especially not when his knees started shaking and he had to sit down on an upturned bucket next to the tractor. That sealed his case.

"You need to get home and go right to bed," she declared in a tone of voice he no longer had the strength to dispute. "Maybe even to the doctor. I'm going to drive you."

"No." He surprised himself at the volume he managed, but he wasn't able to shake her off when he somehow pulled himself to his feet. "I can drive myself."

"Yes, and if you black out on the highway, what then?"

"Not going to happen." He pointed himself in the general direction of Lazarus, hoping he didn't weave too much.

"Pete, I haven't seen you this sick since you had the flu in the fifth grade. Really. I should drive—"

"Mom!" He tried not to raise his voice; it just came out

that way. And he kept walking. "Thanks for the offer. But I can drive myself, all right?"

"At least call me when you get home."

"How about if I don't call, and then you can assume I'm OK."

"You're not OK."

"It's just a little flu. I'll be fine."

"People die from the flu. It's nothing to fool around with."

He paused to fight back another wave of nausea, holding his head. "Tell Dad I'll see him tomorrow."

He hurried to the truck as fast as his wobbly legs would carry him, and he waved gamely at his mom as he pulled away. She was right about one thing. He hadn't been this sick since the fifth grade. And that had been one nasty case of the flu, keeping him in bed for the better part of a week.

Only back then, the worst thing he'd had to worry about was missing school and a little homework. If he remembered correctly, his mom had even brought him home some store-bought spumoni ice cream because he couldn't hold down much of anything else. That and cherry-flavored Jell-O. And chicken noodle soup. That part wasn't so bad. The rest of it, including the bucket by the side of his bed, he would rather forget.

He pressed the accelerator a little more than he should have as he sped down Heather Creek Road toward town, covering the distance in record time. He waved stiffly to Brad Weber, who was probably making a parts delivery and wondering where Pete was headed this time of day.

Home, Brad. Home to bed.

Hopefully none of the neighbors noticed him rolling out of his truck and hobbling past Dana's little car in the driveway. Really, to be safe he probably should have let his mom drive. But all he wanted to do now was tumble onto his bed with a groan.

As he opened up the front door, he was struck by the smell of garlic and onions, and it dawned on him that he had walked past Dana's car. The smell made his stomach turn even more, as did the thought of any kind of food.

"Honey? What's wrong?" Dana's face appeared in the foyer. Like his mom a few minutes earlier, she wore a kitchen apron—this one smeared with tomato sauce. Underneath that she was wearing her nice dark business suit—she hadn't bothered to change. He looked at her and grimaced.

"Guess I caught something," he told her in a pained whisper.

"Caught something? Are you sick?"

"Don't come too close."

But she didn't listen as she helped him slip off his boots and the rest of his dusty clothes; then she walked him toward the bed.

"I'm sorry," she said, and her voice felt as good as anything he could think of. "I've never seen you so ill. Even before the wedding you didn't look this bad."

He held up his hand.

"Sorry," she told him. "That wasn't the nicest thing to say."

"It's all right." He lay back on the pillow, trying to breathe deeply while she took his temperature and then brought him a glass of cool water to sip as well as some kind of grape-flavored liquid for his headache. She laid a folded, cool washcloth on his forehead.

"You're the prettiest nurse I've ever seen," he managed. "But what are you doing here so early in the afternoon anyway?"

"A hundred and one," she answered, checking the thermometer. "If it gets any higher than that, I'm calling Dr. Carr."

Same message, different messenger. Somehow it sounded better when it was Dana doing the nursing, rather than his mom. Even with his insides all knotted up and his head pounding as if it had been through a feed mixer, he didn't mind as much—as long as it was Dana.

"You want more water?" she asked a few minutes later.

"How about a 7-Up?" he replied, curling into a fetal position under the covers. He couldn't decide if he was hot or cold, alternately sweating and shivering. "That's the only thing that sounds good right now."

"Oh, so now I'm taking orders, huh? I assume you're not going to want any spaghetti and meatballs tonight."

He closed his eyes. "You came home to make dinner?"

"Don't act so surprised. I'm allowed to do that once in a while."

"No meetings?"

"None that matter. I skipped out early."

"Really? I thought you liked meetings. Feeling important. Deciding other people's lives. Making the big bucks."

She didn't answer, and he eventually opened his eyes to see if she was still in the bedroom or if she'd retreated back to the kitchen. She stood at the doorway, her arms crossed and a distressed look on her face.

"What?" he asked. "I was just kidding. Really."

"I don't think you were."

"I'm drugged, OK? Delirious. Don't know what I'm saying. I'm sorry."

"No, I'm the one who's sorry."

"Huh?" He blinked his eyes. His head hurt as she explained.

"Sorry that I can't help with the house. Sorry that I don't have time to meet you for lunch anymore. Sorry that I miss all your calls. And sorry that when I get home at night, I'm completely exhausted."

"It's OK."

"No, it's not. And you know what else? I miss my classroom. I miss my kids. I'm sure the sub is doing a fine job, but I keep wondering what's happening, as if I were still responsible for what happens there. But most of all I don't like who I'm becoming."

"No, you're fine. You're . . ."

By this time the medicine had really started to kick in, and he couldn't keep his eyes open. In fact, he must have dropped off to sleep for a while because when he opened up his eyes again, he couldn't see across the dark room. All he could tell was that Dana's hand on his forehead felt soft and cool, and it was the nicest thing he'd felt all day.

"Feel like some chicken soup?" she asked.

"I feel like curling up in a cave and disappearing," he answered. He covered his mouth to cough, and his chest hurt when he did. Apparently this bug covered all the bases, from hacking and headache to everything in between. "Were we talking about something?"

"Actually, you fell asleep five hours ago," she informed him, rising from the bed.

"Oh." His head still throbbed, and it hurt even more when he talked. "But what about your job? I can't remember."

"Never mind, honey. We can talk about it later. I'll heat up some soup for you."

His head felt heavy again, so heavy, as if he were dreaming while he was still awake, or still awake while he was dreaming. He fell back asleep before Dana could return with his soup.

Chapter Twenty-Six

By seven the next morning Charlotte decided she wasn't going to get back to sleep, and that it was too late for that anyway. She dragged her feet to the kitchen, where Bob was helping himself to a cup of coffee.

"Ah, sleeping in on a Saturday, huh?" he ribbed her between sips of coffee. "I thought you were never going to get up."

For a moment she considered telling him she'd been awake since two that morning, tossing and turning and worrying about Pete and Dana's house situation. Of course Bob hadn't lost a wink of sleep over it.

As she set to work making Saturday breakfast she wished she could just compartmentalize her life the way Bob always did. Everything would be so much simpler. She could sleep at night, not worry about her son's troubles. She'd just wake up on Saturday morning and eat breakfast. She stood there on the cool linoleum in her bare feet, sorting through all these things in her mind.

"You don't look too good," Bob finally told her. "You're not catching what Pete has, are you?"

"I'm not catching anything, Bob, but I don't know how you manage not to worry about things."

"Doesn't really change anything if I do," he answered. "You should know that by now too."

Of course he was right, Charlotte conceded to herself as she made his eggs just the way he liked them.

They ate their breakfast in silence, and then Charlotte headed to the bathroom to shower and dress.

She had composed the start of a grocery list in her head, so when she got back to the kitchen she grabbed her purse before heading out the door. Bob still sat at the breakfast table without a care in the world, reading the paper and sipping a glass of juice.

"You sure they'll be open?" he asked, never lowering his paper. "It's still only seven forty-five."

She knew that. But no sense in wasting the day.

"They'll be open."

She pushed through the back door and hurried off.

Charlotte wasn't the only one in the little grocery store at eight fifteen on a Saturday morning. As she rounded the produce aisle with a bundle of bananas in her basket, she nearly ran into her neighbor, Rhonda Freeman, pushing a cart.

"Oh!" Rhonda looked as if she'd just awakened, with her thinning gray hair tucked under a bandanna. Charlotte assumed they shared a similar expression. But it would only be polite to exchange a couple of words.

So Charlotte inquired about the Freemans' grandchildren in St. Louis, and of course they were fine, though one of them apparently had come down with some kind of cold. Charlotte remarked that Pete had as well and that he hadn't looked so sick since the fifth grade.

"I remember that," said Rhonda, pulling out her grocery list. "Wasn't that the time you nearly called an ambulance?"

Charlotte replied that yes it was, and she thanked Rhonda for remembering. And thus with the pleasantries aside, the two women each started to go her own way.

But Charlotte couldn't just let it go. Not after the sleepless night she'd just endured. Bob certainly wasn't going to say anything. It was up to her.

"Rhonda," she blurted out, "there's something I need to ask you."

Since Rhonda had already rolled almost around the corner, they both had to stop and maneuver to face each other again. Charlotte unloaded her speech as quickly as she could before she chickened out or changed her mind.

"I don't know if you've heard what's happened with Pete and Dana's house. But you know it's been their dream, and they're both working so hard. I think Pete's come down sick on account of how hard he's working."

Rhonda could only stare and nod as Charlotte went on.

"And so I was wondering, how hard could it be for you folks to straighten out that misunderstanding about the boundary? I don't bring it up for my own sake or for Bob's —goodness no. I'm only mentioning it because I know that Bob would never say anything, and Pete's a lot like his father that way. You know, they don't like to ask for help, and they don't like to admit there's a problem. But I would just hate for them to lose so much, all on account of an honest mistake. A misunderstanding, really. Do you know what I'm trying to say?"

Goodness, thought Charlotte, *judging by the way she's looking at me, I think I just ruined any chance of fixing this problem.*

As a matter of fact, Rhonda looked a bit confused. She actually cocked her head to the side as she stared back at Charlotte.

"Dear, I'm sure I have no idea what you're talking about. But if it's something Walt needs to work out with your Pete, I'll be sure to pass along the word. Something about the boundary, you say?"

Rhonda smiled sweetly as she examined the broccoli display, leaving Charlotte to stutter an awkward reply.

"Yes, actually, uh . . ." Now she wished she could take back what she'd just spilled, or perhaps start over, a little more slowly. "Never mind. It's probably best to let the boys work this out on their own. I shouldn't have even brought it up. The broccoli's a little old, isn't it?"

Charlotte decided the rest of the items on her list could wait; she really ought to be leaving. Rhonda gave her another puzzled look as Charlotte said good-bye and headed straight for the one open checkout lane.

She decided that from then on she would stick to influencing the kids still in her care—if she still could.

DANA ALMOST FELT she needed to knock at the door to her classroom later that Saturday morning. Her *former* classroom, actually. But not because anyone would be there. Probably the only other people in the entire building would be a couple of janitors and maybe a coach or two, getting ready for that day's track meet. None of the teachers would be there.

Except her.

"Hello?" She couldn't help feeling sad as she pushed inside the empty room, holding her conflicted emotions in check. There on the board, the reading assignment had been neatly printed for Steinbeck's *Of Mice and Men*—but not in her handwriting. She recognized the chapter and recalled a dozen discussions she and her students had had on the part where Curley's hand was crushed.

Her funny posters of Shakespeare and C.S. Lewis still hung on the walls, along with a movie poster for *The Lord of the Rings*. Pete had especially liked that one and had looked for it every time he visited the classroom—when he used to do that sort of thing. She grinned.

"Yes, Mr. Anderson," she remembered telling the boy in the front row on the first day of school, "you will still need to read the book."

The kid hadn't even known there *was* a book. And when she closed her eyes, she could still see the class full of faces, all looking at her with alarm as she read to them from *Othello*. Did Shakespeare really say that?

Well, yes, as a matter of fact. That and a lot of other interesting, confusing, exciting things. Welcome to English lit! She ran her hand along the tops of the desks, thinking of the students she had left behind, praying for them by name as she did. But then she remembered she no longer taught these kids, and it brought her up short.

Is this what you wanted for me, Lord? she asked. *Please show me.*

She could almost hear the voices of her students once again, laughing at the way she'd introduced their reading assignments in freshman composition classes. Remembering the way Bryce Ferguson's face had lit up when he suddenly understood the powerful messages hidden in *To Kill a Mockingbird*. And how Meghan Willow worked so hard on her report on *Cry, the Beloved Country*. Considering the home that petite girl had come from, the report had been a minor miracle.

And now Dana was considering giving all that up. For what? Pete's feverish words still echoed in her mind.

I thought you liked meetings. Deciding other people's lives. Making the big bucks.

She looked out across the empty seats again, searching for answers in her memories of assigned readings and of the young students who had passed through that door.

She really needed to get to the pharmacy this morning, now that it was open. She hoped they had some of that daytime flu medicine rather than the stronger stuff that knocked her poor husband out every time he took it. She stepped out into the hall just as Principal Duncan came striding around the corner.

Again? she wondered. *Seems like every time I stop by after hours, he finds me here.*

"There's my hardworking assistant!" He grinned as he caught up with her. "Checking to see that your sub is keeping things in order?"

"Not exactly," she replied. "Everything I've heard about her has been very good."

"True; she's doing a good job. Which reminds me, we need to go over several teacher evaluations. I know you're not here for that today, but ..."

"Actually, I was on my way to Kepler's. I'm sorry. Pete's been sick."

"Oh! Sorry to hear it."

She noticed that his face fell but guessed it wasn't from hearing about Pete. If he was fishing to see if she would put in extra weekend time, she would have to disappoint him this time. They continued down the hall together, toward the main office and the front entry, and she took a deep breath as Mr. Duncan went on about the teacher evaluations.

What's really most important? she asked herself. After visiting her classroom she knew the answer, and she knew now what she had to say. Better to tell him here than to wait any longer.

"Actually, Mr. Duncan, there is something I need to ask you. I've been thinking about next fall."

"Excellent. You seem to be catching on quickly. I really think you would do a fine job."

"That's just it. I know we've talked about this, but I've been doing some thinking. Some . . . praying. I'm happy to fill in for the rest of this school year. But I don't think I'll be applying for the permanent position after all."

If he'd been disappointed before, it was nothing compared with how he responded now. His eyes widened at the news, and he nearly tripped over his feet as he skidded to a stop in the middle of the hallway.

"What? You're sure about that? I thought you would be perfect for the position. Still do. What made you change your mind?"

She sighed.

"Pete getting sick kind of made me think that I'm missing out on the things I value the most. And right now I really need more time to adjust. Being a farm wife and having a career, well, it's not as simple as I thought. And besides, I really miss the classroom. The kids. I'd really like to be there for them in September. If that's still possible."

They walked along again in silence for a few more paces as a vacuum cleaner hummed somewhere in the distance. Finally he stopped at the main office door.

"You're really sure this is what you want? You and Pete are agreed on this?"

"We've talked about it. And Pete's been really supportive of whatever I want to do. He hasn't been too thrilled about my late hours, but—"

"But you know most of that is just the learning curve, don't you?"

"Sure. But it's more than that. Standing back in my old classroom helped bring things back into focus. I'd really like my old job back. I'm sure this is what I need to do."

"Hmm." Principal Duncan frowned. "I can't say I'm happy to hear this, but I do respect your decision. And you know there's always a classroom for you here."

"Thank you. I appreciate your understanding."

"I didn't say that." Now he was smiling again, sort of. "Now I'm going to have to interview even more candidates for this spot. You *will* sit on the interviewing committee, right?"

"I think I can handle that."

She felt a sense of relief wash over her. As she headed out the front doors she almost felt like skipping all the way home.

First she had to stop at the pharmacy for Pete's medicine.

She hurried through her errand and arrived home in record time.

"Pete!" she called out the moment she stepped inside. "You'll never guess what just happened."

Her patient was lying on the couch in his pajamas, watching a Saturday fishing show on TV. He coughed and looked up at her as if he had something to say himself.

"This mess is all my fault," he told her.

"What mess? I don't see anything. A couple of tissues on the floor maybe, but—"

"No, no." He shook his head. "The mess with the house. I should never have let it happen this way. I assumed way too much, and look what happened. So first thing Monday I'm going to go find Walt Freeman and work this thing out. Should have done it a long time ago."

"Anything I can do to help?" she asked, settling down next to him on the couch and opening up the package from the pharmacy. He gazed at her with eyes at half-mast.

"Not likely. Not with your new job."

"Actually, there's not going to be a new job," she told him.

Chapter Twenty-Seven

Everyone get in the car," Charlotte ordered the kids after an after-church snack of fruit and chips. Sam looked at her like she was crazy, of course, but that didn't deter her one second. She'd planned for every eventuality. "Everybody who comes with me is going to be treated to a dinner of their choice at any restaurant in Grand Island."

"What?" Emily's mouth flapped a little, as if she was trying to find a way out but couldn't. "You didn't warn us about any of this."

"Sorry." Charlotte shrugged the way she'd seen her grandkids do on more than one occasion. "I've been trying to figure out a way to make this work, but I didn't think of all the details until just today."

"What happens if we stay here?" Christopher wanted to know.

"If you stay here, you can have reheated mac and cheese with Grandpa."

Five minutes later they were headed north up the highway on the hour-long drive to Grand Island—Sam in the front seat with her, Christopher and Emily in the back.

"How about that?" She smiled at them in the rearview mirror. "I had a feeling you might want to tag along."

"What are we going for again?" asked Christopher. "I mean, besides Sam's new school?"

"It's not my new school yet." Sam still wasn't giving in. "We're just going there 'cause Grandma wants to."

Charlotte glared at him as sharply as she could.

"And to check it out," he added.

Charlotte realized he needed to make these kinds of decisions bit by bit. So she would help Sam along, just a little. The good news was that she had him to herself for an entire Sunday afternoon so he was a captive audience.

"I hear there's a weather station on campus," she told Christopher. "Maybe we could get in to see it."

"Cool!" It didn't take much to satisfy him. In the seat beside him, Emily sat quietly and texted her friends, thumbs flying across the tiny keyboard on her cell phone. Charlotte decided to leave her alone. Like Christopher, she had probably only agreed to come because of the dinner bribe. But at least she had come along.

"I think you're going to like this campus, Sam," Charlotte told him. She worried that perhaps he still had not completely faced the reality of his coming graduation. He sat with his arms crossed over his chest, staring at the rows of newly plowed fields flashing by. She wondered what was going through his head. Was he upset that he had been coerced by his grandmother into visiting a school he really didn't want to attend? He grunted his reply as she went on, and she felt like she was almost babbling to fill the silence.

"Well, the pictures I've seen of the campus are very nice, and I called to make sure there's someone there to show us around this afternoon."

He grunted again.

"Plus they have a snack bar, an activity center, and all the computer—uh, *information* programs I think you're interested in."

"Information technology." Sam finally filled her in but still kept an eye on the passing farms. "Yeah, I know."

"You sound like someone on TV, Grandma." Christopher was following the conversation, and Charlotte could tell Emily was listening in too, despite her texting. "You could sell the amazing Clean-eeze mop, no problem."

"The amazing . . . Oh, now you're just pulling my leg."

By that time they had reached the outskirts of Grand Island, and she followed the signs onto the Husker Highway, driving just a short way farther until the college campus appeared on the left. Christopher pointed over the seat back.

"I see it!" he said, sounding as excited as Charlotte wished Sam could be. He would warm up to the idea eventually. At least she hoped he would. Emily even looked up from her cell phone long enough to notice where they were as they pulled onto the treed campus and found a visitor parking spot.

"So, here we are!" Charlotte tried to sound upbeat. She knew this could go really well, or not. It all depended on Sam's attitude.

She watched him carefully as they found their way to the main offices and then introduced themselves to an admissions aide. They followed a second-year student named Gary Bertold around on a campus tour. Charlotte thought he was the one she had spoken to on the phone.

"What are you studying here, Gary?" Charlotte asked him. She wasn't above keeping the conversation going. This Gary looked like a very nice young man, not very tall, with friendly eyes and a shy smile. Even Emily seemed to notice.

"Information technology," he told them. "I'm going into programming. I'll show you guys the computer labs next. They're right up here."

What a stroke of luck. Charlotte hung back a little more as the kids started talking computer languages and tech things. Sam even asked a few questions. Charlotte had no idea now what they were saying, but that was perfectly fine with her. Christopher walked with her and Emily, tugging on her sleeve and asking when they were going to see the weather station.

"It's right up here too." Gary looked over his shoulder at them and pointed at a modern-looking two-story building up ahead. He must have heard Christopher's question. "I'm no weather expert, but maybe you can tell us about the equipment."

Christopher beamed at the possibility, even though they would spend the next half hour in the computer labs, speaking with professors and a couple of students, staring at servers and mainframes and heaven knows what else. Charlotte was just as lost there as she might have been at NASA's mission control, but she couldn't keep from smiling as she saw Sam light up for the first time in ages.

"This is very cool," he kept saying, and by that time he

must have forgotten to put on the well-rehearsed disinterested look. Before long he and Gary were chatting and laughing like old friends. Emily even seemed interested.

"You like the computers too?" Charlotte whispered.

Emily shook her head. "I'm just excited about dinner," she admitted.

"Oh? You mean you know where we're going?"

"Absolutely. There's a very cool natural foods restaurant downtown we have to try called the Happy Vegan. I read about it online. You did say we could choose any place we'd like to eat, right?"

Charlotte gulped and nodded. She could imagine the kind of place—and what they might serve. Raw things. Quivering things. Tofu. But a deal was a deal.

"That sounds lovely, dear. And if that's your choice, that's what we'll do."

"But I want a cheeseburger!" announced Christopher, "and I'm hungry."

Well, that should not have been too difficult a request, except that Charlotte guessed cheeseburgers were not on the menu at the Happy Vegan.

"There's a really good burger joint on the way downtown," Gary interjected. "But if Sam wants to catch dinner with me here on campus, maybe we could meet you guys back here in a couple of hours."

Sam nodded his OK, and they agreed to meet him in front of the tech building at seven. That way they could get back on the road to Heather Creek Farm before it got too late and Bob started wondering if something had happened to them.

Well, thought Charlotte after they had thanked Gary for the tour and made their way to the car. *This is going better than I expected.*

MEANWHILE, PETE SAT on the floor of his half-finished dream home, still feeling sick.

Why have I been so afraid to talk with Walt about this mess? he asked himself. But he knew why. He knew Walt would say again exactly what he had said before.

Pete slammed his hand on the plywood flooring, raising a cloud of dust and doing nothing for his frustration.

I was so sure of myself. So sure I had all the answers.

Now it appeared he had none—unless he could talk Walt Freeman into selling. As if that would happen. As he surveyed the framing around him, complete with windows still marked with graffiti, his heart sank all over again, and he felt even sicker at the thought of losing everything.

We can't start over, he told himself. *I blew it, big time.*

And though Dana had gone almost overboard to encourage him about the whole ugly mess, still he wondered if it could be fixed.

What does she think of this fiasco? Does she blame me as much as I blame myself? How could she not?

Now he dreaded facing his workers as he imagined what he might have to tell them.

I thought we were building on Stevenson land, guys, but I didn't check it well enough. Looks like we're out of money, and I'm going to have to let you go.

No! He pounded the plywood again and jumped to his

feet, making his head swim. Though he knew it was all his fault, he also knew he couldn't give up without a fight. So he clenched his fists and marched out toward his truck, determined, for Dana's sake, to try.

He really didn't want to talk to whoever was driving up the lane. Didn't want to have to explain his failures to anybody—not the lumber-supply guy and not the electricians, not the plumbers and not the roofer. Not anyone. If his pickup hadn't been parked in plain sight, he might have hidden behind a nearby pile of two-by-fours instead of standing there, waiting to see . . .

Walt Freeman's truck grinding to a stop.

"Oh, man." Pete groaned, stopping short of his pick-up. "Of all people."

It was too late to do anything but wait as Walt took his sweet time stepping out of his truck. Talk about timing. The two men eyed each other, and Pete nodded at Walt.

"I was just coming to see you, actually." Pete had a hard time reading Walt's deadpan expression, and he guessed Walt might be making the same effort.

"Oh?" Maybe Walt was gloating about making Pete move the house. No telling what he was really up to this time. But Pete knew he had to take the lead in this conversation, and he cleared his throat as he pulled a paper from his back pocket.

"Yeah. Look here. I know we haven't been seeing eye to eye lately, but I wanted you to see this."

He unfolded the yellowed bill of sale as Walt pulled out a pair of reading glasses from the pocket of his flannel work shirt and then squinted at the ripped old document.

"A bill of sale between your dad and my granddad," Pete explained as Walt looked it over even more closely. "For this land here."

After a few moments Walt asked, "How do I know it's real?"

"Aw, come on. You see the signatures."

Walt frowned and rubbed the paper between two fingers, as if testing to see if it was authentic.

"It's legit, okay?" Pete snatched the paper back as he felt his irritation flare.

"You're saying you own this property on account of that old piece of paper?"

Pete shook his head. "Nope."

"Then what?" Walt held up his hands and looked around. "Looks like we're pretty much back where we started."

"Would you let me explain?" Pete raised his voice before coughing, and for a moment he couldn't stop. Finally he gathered his breath. "Tim at the planning office looked into it, and he told me this deal between my grandfather and your dad was never recorded."

"Why am I not surprised?" Walt could get a little sarcastic. "They might have changed their minds."

Pete frowned and went on.

"And he said that as far as he was concerned, the old boundary was still the same. Long story short, legally I'm encroaching on your property, the way you say."

By now Walt was pacing around a pile of lumber, looking rather impatient.

"So what are you going to do about it?" he asked.

Pete waved at the property, at all the work he'd done, at his—and Dana's—dream.

"I want to buy this land all over again, same as my grandfather did. Cash. Swap. I'll give you a fair offer. Either way, I think you'll come out ahead."

As he paced, Walt rubbed the two-day beard on his chin, still looking doubtful. Finally he stopped long enough to hold his hand out.

"Here, let me see that paper again."

Pete handed it over, unsure if the man was going to read it or tear it to pieces. Walt squinted and finally looked up to face Pete again.

"Would have been a whole lot better," he said deliberately, "if you'd come to me right from the start and explained your side of things, plain and clear."

"I tried—"

"No, you didn't. You just charged in here and started bulldozing without ever talking to me like you had all the answers. I don't appreciate the way you did that. And now you think this old piece of paper makes it right?"

Pete felt his cheeks redden in embarrassment at Walt's words.

"I shouldn't have done things the way I did," he said.

"No, you shouldn't have. The thing is, I would have been OK with making some kind of a deal with you and your dad a long time ago. It could have saved us all a lot of trouble."

Pete knew Walt was right, or mostly right. But still he had to know.

"What about now?" Pete asked, feeling as if he had nothing to lose. "Would you still be willing to make a deal?"

At first Walt didn't answer; he just stepped over to

inspect the house. He paused at the vandalized windows, running a finger over some of the graffiti. Funny that Pete had once suspected Walt of doing the damage! Finally Walt turned back toward Pete and shaded his eyes from the morning sun.

"You've got a couple of acres on that corner up north a little farther. It's not worth much, but maybe I could get some use out of it."

Pete had to keep his jaw from dropping to the ground as he joined Walt by the front porch.

"That's not what you said before."

"Yeah, well, quit acting so surprised, or I might change my mind again."

"But—"

"But nothing. I don't intend to lose any sleep over this, or any money either. You'd be wise to look at it the same way and get back to work. Your new wife is looking forward to moving into this place, isn't she?"

"Yes, she is."

Walt stuck out his hand.

"Then do we have an understanding? You keep the house where it is, and we'll work something out. Talk to your dad about it. And if we make a deal . . ."—he handed the old paper back—". . . we're not going to ink it on the back of some napkin or a scrap of old paper, all right?"

Pete paused for just a moment before shaking Walt's rough hand; he still couldn't quite believe what was happening.

Yeah, they had an understanding this time. Sure enough.

SAM WATCHED BEDFORD'S approaching lights from the backseat of Grandma's car. He elbowed his little brother next to him and then pretended not to notice when Christopher snorted and jerked his head awake.

"We're almost home, kid," Sam told him.

Christopher looked up at him with big eyes illuminated for a second by a passing car.

Christopher sat up a little straighter. "You liked that school, didn't you?"

Sam tried to sound cool about the whole thing. But the truth was . . . yeah, he liked it. He liked it a lot. He liked the computer lab. He liked the campus. Even the snack-bar food tasted better than he had expected. And no one was more surprised then he was.

"I guess it wasn't too bad," he answered.

"So that means—"

"That means maybe you're not getting rid of me that easy." He reached over to grab Christopher's neck in a playful grip. "Somebody's got to stick around to keep you out of trouble, right?"

Christopher giggled and tried to tickle him, which led to a sort of rowdy wrestling match in the backseat that ordinarily would have gotten them in trouble with the driver. But when Sam glanced up he saw Grandma's eyes in the rearview mirror.

He could tell she was smiling.

Chapter
Twenty-Eight

S tevensons are tough," Pete mumbled to himself as he peeled himself out of his truck at the work site Monday morning. He was still achy but a lot better than two days ago. "We don't let a little case of the flu stop us."

Especially not with so much work to do. Ha! With the unexpected green light from Walt, it was pedal to the metal once again. But with his head so deep in thoughts and to-do lists, he almost didn't notice Troy Vanderveen scrubbing the side of the backhoe parked behind the building.

"Hey!" At first Pete thought it might be more trouble. Troy meant trouble, right? "What do you think you're doing out there?"

Troy just about jumped out of his skin, as startled as Pete who marched up to set things straight.

"Oh, wow, you scared me there for a minute." Troy forced a lame smile. He wouldn't be smiling when Pete got through with him. "I didn't think you'd be here this early."

"That doesn't answer my question. What the heck are you doing here?" Pete didn't smile back or ease up. And in an instant he understood: here was the guy responsible for the graffiti. The kid was working on the same backhoe that had been tagged with spray paint, wasn't he? This proved it. And now Troy couldn't seem to get the words out.

"Oh, I was just . . . I mean, I thought maybe I could scrub off some of the mess." He held up his steel wool. "See?"

"Guilty conscience, huh?" When Pete came back at him, Troy obviously winced. No mistake about it. The kid was guilty as sin.

Gotcha!

"No, no. You don't understand." Troy seemed to be backpedaling like crazy, trying to reshape his story to save his sorry skin. Let him try. He wouldn't be able to sweet-talk his way out of this.

"Looks pretty obvious to me, Troy."

Troy pressed his lips together, like he was debating whether to confess. After a long pause he sighed.

"All right, I'll tell you what happened here. You need to know, same as everyone else."

"Sure, why not tell me? The backhoe's all decorated with graffiti, along with that pile of windows. Stuff is ruined. Trashed. Care to add anything?"

Pete forgot about his lingering flu and headache for now. Instead he folded his arms over his chest and waited. This had better be good. If it wasn't, he reserved the right to give the sheriff's department another quick call.

One thing he still didn't understand. How did a kid who drove a nice shiny truck get away with this kind of nonsense?

"Look, I'm really sorry, Mr. Stevenson." Troy held out his

hands as if he was really asking for forgiveness. And before Pete could think better of it, he almost believed the kid. "I really didn't know any of this was going to happen. I was just taking some of my friends to see what you were building here. I thought it was a cool house, is all. So we drove out one night, and I was just showing them around. You know."

"No, I really don't know." Pete kept his arms well folded.

Troy looked good and nervous by this time, digging the toe of his boot into the dirt and moving his jaw around as if he were chewing something.

Guilty, guilty, guilty, thought Pete. The kid wouldn't even look Pete in the eye as he went on with his tall tale.

"Well, here's the thing." Troy pointed over to the far side of the building, the side facing the neighbor's property. "We were over there, and I was just showing one of my friends around, right? But I didn't know my other friend was back here tagging all this equipment and these windows, and making a total mess."

"You've got that part right. Total mess. Still is."

"If I'd known, I would never have let him, for sure."

"Oh, so you just didn't see, huh?" Pete wasn't buying it —not quite.

"That's right. You can believe me, Mr. Stevenson, or not. I'm just really sorry. But when I got back here and saw what was going on, I grabbed his spray can right away and stopped him."

"Yeah? This a friend of yours?"

"Was."

"Does he have a name?"

Troy didn't answer, and started back in on his scrubbing. Pete had to admit it looked a little better already. Some of the lettering had even almost disappeared. He'd been so caught up with the property line, with adjusting to married life and fighting off this cold, that he hadn't really even tried to clean the mess.

"No name," answered Troy in a low voice. "I just wanted to try to make it right—that's all."

"So you ran away? You thought that would make it right?"

"I panicked. I'm sorry. I didn't know what to do."

"Hmm. And now you think you can make it all better with some elbow grease. I called the sheriff about this right after it happened, you know."

"I know." Troy kept up his vigorous scrubbing, back and forth and around and over again. "Like I said, I'm really sorry, Mr. Stevenson."

Pete definitely wasn't used to anybody calling him Mr. Stevenson, and he also wasn't used to seeing such a big kid eating so much humble pie. It made him pause for a moment and reminded him of himself yesterday.

Sort of.

"That still doesn't make it right," Pete told him. "Saying you're sorry isn't like declaring bankruptcy, where every-body just throws up their hands and says, 'Oh, well. I'm sorry, and I can't do anything about it.' There're always consequences, you know. And if you drive the getaway car, you're just as guilty as the guys who robbed the bank. Or in this case, the guys who spray-painted my equipment. You understand?"

"Sure, I understand. But now you want me to do something else? Like pay you a fine or something?"

"I didn't say that."

"You're not going to call the cops again, are you? 'Cause if you do, well, maybe that's your business. But I'm not going to tell you more about him than I already did. And no names."

Pete let him scrub awhile longer, but then he had to know.

"All right," he said. "You're not ratting on your friend, or your ex-friend. I understand that. But does he know you're here, taking all the blame for him?"

Troy shook his head no.

"Nobody knows anything."

"But why did he do it?" Pete asked. "At least tell me that. What did he have against me?"

"Nothing. He doesn't even know you."

"Then what? That's crazy. Are your friends just into random vandalism? I thought that was just in the big cities, not in Bedford. You've got to have a clue."

Pete waited out another long silence before Troy finally opened his mouth again.

"Emily," he finally admitted. "It's because of Emily."

"What?" Pete felt his face flush with anger as his voice rose. He could have strangled the kid just then. "Don't you try to blame Emily for any of this, because if you—"

"No, that's not what I meant. Please. It's not her fault. It's just because of her."

"That doesn't make any sense."

"I know it doesn't. But they think she's a stuck-up Goody Two-shoes."

"Wait a minute. I've never heard my niece described quite that way. Lots of other ways, but not like that."

"Well, I'm just telling you what they think, not what *I* think. They just thought they were doing me a favor by sabotaging my chances with her. They thought I'd get blamed, and then her grandparents—or maybe even you— would tell her she couldn't see me anymore."

"Your friends really think Emily is too good for you, huh? And that makes a difference to you?"

"Of course it does." Troy shrugged as he kept up his scrubbing.

"Wow," said Pete. "With friends like that . . ."

"I haven't been hanging around with them lately, OK?"

"Hmm. So what are you doing this for?"

"I told you. I like Emily. And when she asked me to have dinner with you guys, you know, with the whole family? I saw how nice everybody was. And it made me feel really bad when you guys were talking about . . . you know . . . this stuff here."

Troy finally finished scrubbing one side of the backhoe and went on to the next. Actually, Pete was surprised at how much of the spray paint Troy had been able to remove. If a guy didn't know where to look, he might not even notice. Maybe those windows had a chance after all.

"You're not going to call the cops, right?" Troy asked again.

"I told you—"

"I'm just asking."

"Well I'm telling you that we don't have to call the cops, but that depends on your attitude. You can't just tell me you're doing the right thing, and expect everybody to believe it all of a sudden."

"I'm not just saying it, Mr. Stevenson."

In a crazy sort of way Troy's story actually started to make sense. And as he watched Troy work he came up with a plan.

"All right. I won't call the cops, and in fact I won't tell anybody else—on one condition."

"Nobody else?"

"Nobody else means nobody else. I'll leave it up to you if you want to make any more confessions."

"What's the condition?"

Troy looked expectantly at Pete, who wasn't going to spill all the details . . . just yet.

Let the kid squirm a little, thought Pete. *After all the headaches he's caused, a little squirming won't hurt him.*

"All I'm going to tell you right now is that it's a little bit of real-life restitution, and it won't do you any harm. In fact, it'll be good for you."

"Sounds like I don't have much choice."

"As a matter of fact, you don't. Now get yourself to school before you're in more trouble than you already are. I'll get back to you on the restitution thing."

For the first time all morning, Pete almost felt like smiling.

Chapter Twenty-Nine

T his is what I meant by *restitution*, kid." Pete wanted to smile but kept a game face. "You break something, you replace it. You steal something, you pay for it—plus a bit more on top of that, in most cases."

"Yeah, I get it." Troy removed his ball cap and wiped the sweat from his forehead. The Shelter for Nebraska house was coming together pretty well that Saturday morning, even with all the confusion of volunteers and trucks and kids running around with dripping paintbrushes. "This would be the 'bit more' part."

"Did I say it was going to be easy?"

"You didn't say anything. But look, I'm not complaining. I had it coming."

Pete grinned at the way things were turning out with Troy. He really wasn't such a bad kid once you got to know him. Sure, he'd gotten mixed up with the wrong crowd, and yeah, he'd made some mistakes. But nothing that couldn't be fixed. Besides, in just a few hours here at the Shelter for Nebraska project, Troy had proven himself to be a pretty hard worker. Pete had even thought of hiring him to help on his own house project if things worked out. They would talk about it later.

Sam, on the other hand, looked a bit distracted over in the other corner of the house; he and Arielle and a half-dozen other kids were supposed to be painting the exterior trim of the modest, one-story home. But Pete couldn't tell if Sam was doing more painting or talking with his girlfriend.

"WHY DIDN'T YOU tell me this before?"

Sam watched the tan paint dribble down the handle of his paintbrush, not caring much one way or the other. Arielle kept swishing her brush back and forth along her section of the Shelter for Nebraska project even though she had run out of paint several brushstrokes earlier. She didn't even look at him as she answered his question.

"I hadn't decided until just the other day, Sam. I was waiting for the best time to tell you. Please don't take it personally."

"Personally? That's not it. I just wish, I mean, if you go to Omaha this fall I'll hardly ever see you again. That's nearly four hours away?"

"But it's still in Nebraska, not like Minnesota, right?"

"That's supposed to be good news, that you decided not to go to Minnesota?"

"I'll be home for holidays, no problem. Maybe even for weekends. And I promise I'll e-mail you all the time. I promise."

Sam returned to his painting, feeling just a little sick to his stomach but still looking for options. Maybe he hadn't lost her completely—yet.

"Sam, please," she told him. "I care about you. I just have

to do what I think is best. What I think God wants me to do."

Somehow he couldn't argue with that.

"How do you know that's what God wants you to do?" he asked, toning it down a bit. The kids over to his right were beginning to stare.

"I'm not sure I can answer that. I just know that Grace University is the best fit for me. The program was exactly what I was looking for, plus there're Bible classes too. I'm excited, Sam. Can't you be excited with me?"

He paused and looked over at her, and now he couldn't resist her shy smile. He had never been able to. As fast as it took to explain, his heart melted by several degrees.

"Sure I can," he finally told her. "I'm excited when you're excited. You know that. But I'll tell you one thing. You might have me visiting your campus pretty soon."

Now she beamed and finally dipped her paintbrush back into the bucket.

"I'd be disappointed if you didn't."

"YOU SURE THEY GOT the message to be here?" Bob shifted on his heels as he turned on another set of floodlights, perched like long-necked prehistoric animals to illuminate the framework of Pete and Dana's new home.

"They'll be here," replied Charlotte. "Won't they, Dana? I told them to come as soon as they were finished with their work project. Don't go home; just come here for dessert. That's what I told them."

"They'll be here," Dana reassured them. "Pete told me

they would. After all, Mom's cookies and ice cream? No question about it."

Charlotte knew it had been a long day for Pete and the kids, and then a drive home from Harding, but the good news from that week called for a celebration. The house would be built right here after all!

It hadn't taken much to convince Dana a celebration was in order. And celebrate they would, with chocolate chip-oatmeal cookies and homemade vanilla ice cream, still cranking in the ice cream maker plugged into an extension cord. Bugs and a few moths had discovered the bright work lights in the gathering dusk, but that mattered little.

At last the little convoy of vehicles bumped up their gravel lane carrying Pete and Troy in Pete's old truck, plus Sam and Arielle in Sam's little sports car.

Christopher pointed out the headlights while Emily looked on expectantly. Apparently when someone mentioned Troy's name it hadn't taken much to convince her to come.

The house's framework looked quite festive out there in the middle of the Nebraska farmland, all lit up as bright as day and decorated with several colored birthday balloons Charlotte had been saving. The cheery oasis of light brought them all together to the folding table Bob had set up and the desserts Charlotte had prepared for them.

"What's this all about?" asked Pete as he stepped out of his truck. "I thought I was going home to take a shower, after the way Troy worked me all day, but Dana said I had to come here."

"Me?" Troy joined in the joking. "You were the one with the whip, making us work like crazy."

That set off the laughs for their little impromptu celebration, as the warm May day cooled off around them and caused Charlotte to tug on the shoulders of her light plaid sweater. Even so, Pete and Dana obliged everyone with a brief tour, taking them from unfinished room to unfinished room with a flourish. Troy surprised them by announcing that he'd been offered an after-school job, helping Pete finish the house.

"And who knows?" said Pete. "If the kid works out, I might have him stick around, since I might have some work for him around the farm."

Charlotte didn't miss the spark that passed between them when Emily looked at him.

"Oh, and did everybody hear?" Charlotte made the announcement, pointing at Emily. "This girl passed the test today and got her official Nebraska state driver's license." They all clapped at that bit of good news.

"Do we have anything else to celebrate?" Charlotte asked.

Arielle looked at Sam before she explained about Grace University, and it was easy to see just how excited she was.

"That's wonderful, dear," Charlotte congratulated her.

"Yeah, but what about the ice cream?" asked Christopher. Charlotte took the hint and plopped generous scoops of the fresh ice cream into their plastic bowls.

This time Charlotte knew the cookies had turned out right. Perfect, in fact—just like tonight. Even with the changes that came with each passing year, the comings and the goings, the new friends and the growing up, the ingredients were all here—and finally in the right proportions.

"Good idea, Char." Bob shuffled a little closer to where Charlotte stood, watching the young people in her life. Pete and Dana now wandered arm-in-arm through the shadows of their future kitchen, sharing secrets and looking happier than they had since the wedding. Emily and Troy followed Sam and Arielle through the framed rooms, chatting and joking, exploring every corner. Christopher tagged along with the dog, getting in everyone's way— though no one seemed to mind this time.

"Can I bring back a cookie for Magic?" Christopher asked Charlotte. "I think he's eating more now."

"Well, I don't know if sheep like chocolate chip-oatmeal cookies," she answered. "But maybe one wouldn't hurt."

So he grabbed one and stuffed it in his jeans pocket before rejoining the others. And without anyone else noticing, Bob slipped up to squeeze Charlotte's hand in a way that told her he loved her and that . . .

Everything's going to be just fine.

And she believed him.

About the Author

Robert Elmer is a former pastor and small-town newspaper editor who began writing novels during evenings and weekends, often after the rest of the family was asleep. Today he has written more than fifty books for youths and adults, including *The Duet*, *The Celebrity*, *The Recital*, and *Like Always*. He enjoys speaking at schools, serves on the editorial board of the Jerry B. Jenkins Christian Writers Guild, and lives with his wife, Ronda, near a beautiful lake in rural Idaho. Find out more at www.RobertElmerBooks.com.

A Note from the Editors

Guideposts, a nonprofit organization, touches millions of lives every day through products and services that inspire, encourage and uplift. Our magazines, books, prayer network and outreach programs help people connect their faith-filled values to their daily lives. To learn more, visit www.guideposts.com or www.guidepostsfoundation.org.